GRACE LAKE
a novel by
GLEN HUSER

Glen Huser
July 12, 1990.

NeWest Press

First Edition

Canadian Cataloguing in Publication Data

Huser, Glen, 1943
  Grace Lake, (Nunatak Fiction II)
  ISBN 0-920897-69-X (pbk.)
  I. Title II. Series

PS8565.U84G7 1990   C813'.54   C90-091264-2
PR9199.3.H88G7 1990

Credits

Cover design: Diane Jensen
Editor for the Press: Aritha van Herk
Author photo courtesy of Doran Clark Photography
Cover photo: Sima Khorrami
Printing and binding: Hignell Printing Limited, Winnipeg
Financial assistance:
    Alberta Culture
    The Canada Council
    The Alberta Foundation for the Literary Arts
    NeWest Institute for Western Canadian Studies
Printed and bound in Canada

NeWest Publishers Limited
Suite 310, 10359 - 82 Avenue
Edmonton, Alberta
Canada   T6E 1Z9

This is a book of fiction and all characters are fictional.

My special thanks to Aritha van Herk and Rudy Wiebe for their help in shaping this work. I would also like to thank the members of my writing workshop—and English 584—who read *Grace Lake* in its several draft stages. Gratefully acknowledged is the financial assistance extended by the Alberta Heritage Scholarship Fund.

for Karen

We shall not cease from exploration
And the end of all our exploring
Will be to arrive where we started
And know the place for the first time.

T.S. Eliot

ONE

His last summer at Grace Lake, John Hislop takes the road he has always taken to get to the camp, a gravelled highway that runs along familiar fields, past sloughs and other small lakes before winding its way through the hills flanking the Beaver River. On maps it has a number, but he thinks of it as the McAllister Road. He has forgotten if McAllister was the name of one of the first farmers, or an early postmaster, or a place remembered by some homesick homesteader. Has he ever known? A faint dust, a talc of clay hangs in the air, exhaled from the ditch-grass and low-lying bushes. It leaves a layer of fine powder over the black '51 Ford, but still the chrome catches the sunlight and winks at him. Mrs. Washburne washed and polished it the day before. You let me do it, she said, barricading herself with pails and torn sheeting. Keep your heart rested. She said heart without the h. Art. He must have smiled, the smile as vestigial as her Cockney accent. Aggrieved, she pinned him with black eyes. Some may mock. It's sheer foolishness going out there this year as if the place would collapse if you missed a summer. Each word ascending to a higher register, ending in a tremolo of indignation.

Not much has changed along the road. Old farmhouses sink a bit more into the ground, their unglazed windows staring out from sockets of rotting wood. In past years there had been times when he felt compelled to stop, to wade through the weeds, to touch his fingers against the husked edge of the sills and peer in at the bleached and tattered wallpaper, the scribbled obscenities of invaders. Nearby, on a road that he travels even less than the McAllister Road, the house that sheltered him through childhood has become one of the same vacant-eyed derelicts, settling itself slowly to the earth.

The county has cut back the ditch growth along the road, chokecherry and saskatoon bushes giving way to pitch-stained poles with their lines strung across the sky like unfilled music stanzas. There were no poles, no telephones, no electricity twelve years before when they first set up the Grace Lake camp. The cabins are still without power, but the large mess hall was wired three— maybe four— summers ago. Will you be needing this lantern, then? Earlier that morning, Mrs. Washburne emerged from the cellar, a goddess gone awry, cobwebs on her bandana, triumphantly holding a camp lantern. The battery-sparked light flashing on and off and on again, a beacon in her extended arm. It went into a box in the trunk of the car. Her hands, stubby, water-reddened, rearranging his books, the other bits of camp gear, finding a corner, tucking, smoothing, arranging. She thrust a red lard pail at him as he got into the car. Just a few egg sandwiches and rhubarb tarts. You've had your heart in the hospital, she reminded him. All illnesses, it seems, are improved by the consumption of food.

Out of the corner of his eye he can see the lunchpail resting on the floor in front of the passenger seat. It becomes a piece in a pattern, one of many patterns that lately tease his mind. The red lard pail seems to be the same one he used to carry his lunch to school when he was a child, although, of course, it can't be. Soft bread cut in triangles, the fused line of jam, the folds of waxed paper, details dot his mind like the black dots in a child's painting book, those strange books where, with the brushing on of water, hidden colours emerge, patterns congeal.

The drive to Grace Lake takes two hours

along the McAllister Road. He had planned to leave early enough that he would be able to spend an hour at the Carey place on the crest of the river hills and still make the administration meeting at two. No need to hurry. Reverend Tupper's hand heavy on his shoulder. Just make it when you can. We're glad you're still on the team. Religion for Frank Tupper is something like a volleyball game. Serve, that's the key word. It's your serve; keep the ball in the court; keep it in play. Smight, before him, had gone in for construction analogies. People's lives as houses for God. Strong foundations and good drains.

It was Smight who established the camp, who first convinced him that he should join as a counsellor. A change of pace. The phrase rested in Smight's mouth alongside bits of Mrs. Washburne's pound cake, served with Sunday coffee. You need a change of pace, John. It's no good spending your whole life in a parlour, now and then peeking out through curtains and glass. You need to get out and take down the storm windows and shingle the roof and feel the Lord's good sun on your neck. The voice he remembered, the smooth assertive voice, framed with certainties.

He went with Reverend Smight to the Grace Lake site, felt the sun on his neck and the wind from the lake against his face. He saw the islands anchored against the horizon and heard the loons' quavering calls in nights soft and black, nights shot with moonlight. He came again the next year. The summers run together in his mind except for that one summer, clear and separate, the summer that the Dejarlais boy rode to camp with him, a sunny and cloudless July day with the same heat and powdery dust. The images, the sounds, the smells of the past fold over and adhere. The two of them laughing as they hurried to get the car windows rolled up whenever a vehicle showed itself in the rear-view mirror or approached them on the stretch of road ahead. Not that there was ever much traffic on the McAllister Road, the odd pickup truck, clumsy tractors lugging farm machinery. Laughter came more easily than talk to them. He can hear the laughter of the boy, cracking to a deeper register only to be chased by the nervous giggle of the child. It is a faint presence in the car, faint and wavery like the heat itself. He'll be a bit of company on the way out, Reverend Smight said. Do the lad good to get away from that environment, you know. The minister's lips curling on that, peeling up over his teeth as if he had bitten into something gone bad.

He drives until the sun is at its highest, radiative and diffuse in the sky's core. Sometimes on the trip, of course, it rains. In the rain, the contours of the valley soften, the green smoulders. But today the sun is out and there is not a cloud anywhere. The valley blazes and the sluggish, shallow river catches some of the sky, shivering with light before slipping back to its dark, jackfish green.

He eats half of one of Mrs. Washburne's sandwiches, sitting on a stump by the Carey cellar. You don't eat enough to keep a bird alive, she likes to remind him, whisking in trays of food, plates helmeted with enameled mixing bowls, buns wrapped in white cloth. Out of the red lard pail there is a smell that mixes with the heat, a hint of sulphur and vinegar. From around the sandwich a piece of waxed paper escapes, fluttering into the cellar hollow. There is no house anymore, just the cellar overgrown to grass, lapping the sides of what has been a cookstove, now settled to rust. Rust in peace. Lungwort clusters along one edge of the indentation, its skim-milk bells dangling and still in the warm envelope of midday. But past, and he just spots it now, there are pinkish stalks of elephant head. Just one clump. It is unusual to find elephant head so far from the foothills.

He removes the tarts from the lard pail and puts in three stalks to press later. One of the blossoms comes off in his hand and he lets it sink into the well of his palm, glandpink against his whiteness, the mastodon features replicated in the corolla. Even the trunk. Even the tusks. The Careys couldn't have transplanted it here. He would have noticed it before. Larkspur had been Mrs. Carey's favourite, or bleeding heart. If he looked, he might still find a clump anchoring some forgotten corner of the yard.

A great gardener. That's what people said about Mr. Carey before they moved into a whispered discussion of his wife's insanity. Crazy as a cuckoo. From where he eavesdropped as a child, his mother serving tea to one of the towns-women, he had plucked the phrase and savoured it. It ripened in its rightness over the years. Mrs. Carey would have loved nothing more than a cuckoo clock, with its hidden bird, the whirr of springs, the startled calls. Both of the Careys were dead now, of course, but he had seen Mrs. Carey a few years ago when he went to visit his grade five teacher, Mrs. Swenson, in the Sunset Arms, the two old ladies like thistles gone to seed. Both of them in wheelchairs. You're Jackie Hislop. Mrs. Carey's voice flirting with private laughter. Flower boy, she giggled, spittle bubbling at her sunken mouth. Flower boy. What do you mean, Edith? Mrs. Swenson squeezing the wrinkles of her eyesocket into a wink at him.

When had Mrs. Carey died? The sun comes warm and still. Hornets settle on Mrs. Washburne's tarts, on the beads of larded syrup drawn by the heat. Flower boy. How odd. When had she begun calling him that? He closes his eyes. There is never complete blackness, more like a red dark. The poplar leaves rustle even when there is no breeze. The heat of the sun on his face, the healing sun. Would it help against his chest if he peeled his shirt off? Heal the heart? He had never been one to expose his skin. In summer, he undid the top button of the longsleeved cotton shirts with their Mrs. Washburne creases along the sleeves. Hide the soft white. The boy had taken off his shirt, though, and moisture slicked his torso, making rivulets along the cattail brown of his skin, welling in his navel. Dark curls of hair beginning to form in the armpit. His arm flung behind his head. Chewing on a piece of foxtail, white teeth flashing. The shy laugh. He can hear it now like a whisper in his ear, a caress of sound. It makes his heart race.

And yet he is resting. Take it easy. Lots of rest. A little sun. Dr. Grodey's advice, cryptic, disseminated with pills, his eyes never leaving the file, his pen moving methodically along the course of some mystical inventory. Only at the end, a flourish, a looking up. We can't easily replace you, you know. I expect some good sense.

A man of science.

Later Mrs. Washburne quizzed him. What did the doctor say? If you ask me, you're too much over those lessons. It hunches you over, it does, and cramps your inner organs. All them up and down scales, hours and hours at the Legion. Was she once a nurse's aide? He hasn't paid attention. Perhaps during the war. Her admonitions tremble with the righteousness of near-medicine. Sometimes they bring a terrible, almost uncontrollable laughter boiling up from inside him so that he has to rush to the washroom and turn the water on. I seen a liver once, all twisted and scrunched like a Parkerhouse roll. They said it come out of a hunchback.

The gentle red dark of noon on the river hills

settles over him like a blanket. His eyes are
closed but he can't give in to sleep. Just a rest,
the elephant head still clinging to his palm, his
hands in his lap, his back against a tree-stump.
Why Grace Lake? You've done your time there. A
trace of a smile on the doctor's lips, the file
closed, looking at the fountain pen in his hand as
if considering the wisdom of adding more ink to
the pages in the manila folder. Not my idea of a
holiday, I can tell you. But he doesn't try to
explain, settling himself against the inadequacy
of words, the bolsters of silence. Too easy to offer
the small lies of rhetoric. They skim like mayflies
over the surface of something as heavy and
amorphic as water. The balances of pain and
pleasure. Dr. Grodey's question teases, makes
him call to mind strange inventories. A six-year-
old taking him by the hand and leading him out
into the lake where he had discovered a perfect
water lily. The touch of the child, the still, heavy
water, the waxen gold of the plant's petals. For
some reason, it is what he thinks of first. Balance
that against—what? The bone-weariness after a
full day's program? No. Generalities should not
be ledgered across from the specific. Choose the
crawling minutes of the long nights when there is
no sleep. Choose the mirror image of the grey
face in the night window. Choose the boy curled
into the wet moss, crying, shuddering.

Mr. Carey had died at the wheel of his car, he
remembers. They found the car still running
against the side of Whittier's barn as if it were

trying to grind into it, and Mrs. Carey sitting in the passenger seat holding her purse primly in her lap. For a while, when he was still in the hospital, it seemed like he had misplaced some of his memories, but he is finding them again, in the same way that one stumbles across a lost pair of glasses at the back of a bureau drawer. It has been a long time since he thought about the Careys. Or Roy Dejarlais. The night the boy was missing from his bed. The sound of his own fist pounding on the door to Reverend Smight's room. Who is it, Bertrand? Mrs. Smight's voice high in the night.

He's not asleep. Not in his bed.

Smight rubbing sleep out of his eyes, licking sleep off his teeth.

Flashlights crisscrossing in the dark.

Just a bit of light on the face there, now. Dr. Grodey's eyes are those of a bird alert to sudden prey. The ceiling is portioned into tiles, bonewhite, porous. But the light has made spots of red dance across them. Should he pray? Elsie Panek, the nurse, squeezes his shoulder. A nurse called Panek; he laughs somewhere inside his mind where it won't intrude on the colony of pain in his chest. His breath becomes a series of frail, guttural escapes. It seems to come from someone else. An old man wheezing.

That night Smight's breath came in gasps, the rattle of a smoker pushed to sudden action as they fought their way through tangles of brush, the flashlight wobbling, catching a tree branch, a clump of marsh grass, a stalk of fireweed, a startled owl, the boy. *Thank God, Smight barely able to form words through his struggle for air, I thought the lake.*

Roy? Are you alright? Reaching down, his own hands flashing through the light beams toward the wet dark-matted hair, the stained cheek, the naked shoulder. He can see them moving, large, long-fingered, almost separate beings. Moving through the light, slower and slower, like a movie when the film breaks and garbles to a stop. Each hand has a ten-key span, thumb to little finger. *I wish I had your hands, old man.* That was what Malcolm said, watching him practice, watching him stalk up and down the keyboard on tenths. Malcolm's own hands draped over the scarred upright in the practice room, a cigarette dangling from his thin fingers. He remembers hands, the tobacco stains along the inside of Malcolm's second and third fingers, a slight splaying out of the little finger. The twisted left hand of the young counsellor, the hymn-singing counsellor, who had been at the camp for a couple of years. He can remember the hand held close to the chest like a small wounded animal, a bird, but he can't remember the counsellor's name.

Was it two summers ago at camp that they had taken canoes and gone to one of the small islands overnight? A cloudless night when the stars seem to move closer to the earth, and they stayed up to let the fire die out. All around them the boys lay quiet in their bedrolls and the night was still except for the nocturnal, muted sounds of frogs, the call of a night bird.

What would make you want to go back to Grace Lake? Dr. Grodey had asked.

A water lily in the hand of a child. A young counsellor humming softly. *Come home, come ho-o-ome; ye who are weary come home.* Mrs. Carey, too, had liked to sing hymns. She would break into them in the middle of a visit to their farmhouse, sing a couple of lines or a verse and then move her fingers coyly to her mouth. Oh my, whatever does get into me? It was said that when Albert Carey felt the urge to get into her, she warbled continuously and so distracted him that he wasn't always able to finish his business. Where would such a story come from?

He has lost track of the time, resting, half-dozing against the tree, remembering a time before he had ever gone to school when he would lie on the grass of their small orchard and watch the sky, the skittery summer clouds, the branches of the apple trees. The world, he felt, was made for him. The sun, the white butterfly exploring the cluster of yarrow by his cheek, the hawk hovering high above.

TWO

After turning off the McAllister Road, he drives slowly, barely crawling over the dips and turns of the last mile leading into Grace Lake. The ruts seem to change little from year to year and he has a sense of where they will scrape against the bottom of the Ford. Grass grows along the middle of the trail and aspens clamour against its edges, in places brushing against the windshield and even against his face from the open side window. He watches for the moment when the lake will reveal itself, that first, dizzying glimpse of water, incandescent, blinding, stretching across his breadth of vision. When it comes, the world seems to turn and the car races along a field road as if drawn by some force. The gravity of water. The sky is dimished, the lake swells, the buildings of the compound grow larger, more definite.

He knows he is late for the meeting and by the time he has parked and made his way into the mess hall, Tupper's voice, the voice of the administrator, seeps officiously from the staff-room door. Waiting for a pause, he looks out the hall window to the parking lot, a small island of gravel levelled against the grassy slope to the lake. The Ford's shine is now well subdued by a scrim of dust. Is there any use in telling you not to touch this vehicle? Mrs. Washburne, red-faced with exertion, rubbing at a fender with an old towel. It don't need to shine out there anyways, not like it should in town.

The window is a fickle mirror of the hall, the doorway behind him, offering and then withdrawing a flash of plywood, a corner with a strip of molding. Someone is at the doorway, easing her way awkwardly into the corridor in an attempt to pull away from the tar-baby of words. The woman, he realizes, retreating crablike and uncertain on canvas sneakers, is Mrs. Steinhauer, the camp cook. Her apron ties nestle in the dark print of her dress. He recognizes her before she recognizes him. Has the illness changed him that much then?

"Oh," she gasps, "Mr. Hislop." Her voice has the flannel-edged loudness of someone who is missing most of her teeth. She has a mixture of German and Cree blood, he remembers, a smoothskinned stolidity. "How are you feeling?" She lowers her voice to a loud whisper. "They been looking for you."

"Jack." Frank Tupper is at the door, offering teeth-rows of congeniality, the thick hand of welcome. "You made it. Great to see ya, guy. Team's all here." The phrases are dribbled like a basketball. Releasing its hold, the hand then grips his shoulder, propelling him into the staff room, a small flurry of greetings, words rising, flapping, settling. Phil Bragge, the swimming instructor, half-rises and then settles his bulk back into his chair. Adeline Tupper beams over her knitting.

"Now, let's see," Tupper rubs at his chin, "who don't you know? Shirley Stickles." A girl with horn-rimmed glasses like his own, smiling over crooked teeth. "Here to look after the arts and crafts classes, and Terry McEvoy is going to give Phil a hand with the swimming." A young man in a t-shirt and running shorts, his exposed skin already baked brown.

Nothing much has changed in the small staff lounge except for the plywood looking older, darker, more waterstained. Flypaper coils from the ceiling. There is a new calendar on the wall. Krawchuk's Red and White: a boy, a grandfather and a dog at a fishing hole— all asleep in the sun. Generations in comfort and warmth, secure relationships. Tupper has asked him a question. "Just whatever you feel up to, Jack." They are all looking at him. "We'd be quite happy to have you just take a Bible lesson or two and tinkle the ivories for a singalong when it's raining, but. . . . "

"I'll take North Cabin as usual." The drive has been tiring. He is grateful that the young swimming instructor has leapt out of the easy chair to sit on a bench beside the crafts teacher.

"We'll give you the older boys, then. Not so rambunctious."

The meeting drifts back to scheduling. He sinks farther into the chair. Reverend Tupper is at his most fulsome, with chart paper and a blackboard and a wooden pointer which he uses as if conducting a symphony. The wand points at Miss Stickles and she begins talking about the crafts. Pine cones and papier-mâché and pressed paper plates. Wall plaques formed out of burned matches. That will appeal— all boys like fire. Mrs. Steinhauer has returned and collapsed instantly into sleep, her head sunk on her calico bosom, her mouth puckered, open. There is a faintness of snoring, flies, some still free of the coils, buzzing. Adeline Tupper knits, her arms even heavier than he remembers them, her fingers moving deftly, automatically, lime green wool spilling into her lap. Above her left shoulder, a faded Christ holds a lantern and raps at a door. *The Light of the World.* It was one of the master paintings they studied at college and he only remembers it because he thought at the time that the figure bore a striking resemblance to Malcolm Fairchild.

Not that Malcolm had a beard. But the gaunt face, the auburn hair. Something. Phil Bragge rumbles phlegm in his throat, says a few words about the swimming schedule. Amazing that he can still swim, a man his size. The young assistant adjusts his shorts, crosses his brown, gleaming legs, points the toe of his running shoe straight up. Frank Tupper, actually balancing on the toes of his tennis shoes, is talking about the team again and then handing out clipboards to everyone except Mrs. Steinhauer.

Each clipboard contains a register. Some of the names seem familiar but actual faces and figures are elusive. Is that part of the sickness, the loss of exact associations, or has he ever remembered their names? Some, of course. Roy Dejarlais. The boy with a grapestain birthmark on one cheek: Marvin Pilot. Blaine Schultz, one of his piano students. How long since Schultz was at camp? Maybe five years ago. On talent night he played *The Robin's Return*, the piece he had been practicing all that spring. The eternal spring, the eternal robin, young fingers stumbling over the broken chords. The piano is always out of tune after sitting through the lakeside winter. Some years it is worse than others. They can phone, now that they have the phone connection, for the piano-tuner to come from St. Paul. There was no phone at the camp that summer when the boy took so sick. Lying in the moss.

Tupper's voice shifts into prayer. " . . . in the bosom of Your bounty. Help us as we help one another in this Thy work. Let us mold the young mind; let us build the young body."

Roy Dejarlais.

"Let us enter into activities in the spirit of joy."

Adeline Tupper sighs, her fingers dipped in the green nest in her lap. The phlegm in Phil Bragge's throat becomes too much and he clears it, waking Mrs. Steinhauer. She smooths the apron across her stomach, casts her eyes down at her soiled canvas shoes. Shirley Stickles runs a finger along the crease of her slacks with one hand and, with the other, tries to keep her glasses from slipping off the prayer incline of her face. Terry McEvoy uncrosses his legs, flexing the muscles as he resettles them.

The ended prayer pools into quietness. As they leave the lounge for the hall porch, Adeline comes over to him. "How are you, Jack?" she whispers, grabbing his hand and pressing it for an instant before letting it go. The gesture has made a tangle of her needles and yarn.

He shrugs. "Dr. Grodey seems convinced that I'm still part of the world of the living."

"What a scare you gave us." She has stuffed everything back into her knitting bag, covering her clumsiness with a trill of laughter, almost musical laughter. A good singing voice, Adeline Tupper.

"You knitting something for Frank?"

"Oh Lord, no!" The laughter explodes. "This'll be a sweater for Donna's youngest if I ever get it finished." She is a grandmother. He has forgotten. A largeboned woman, she is one of the few women taller than himself, although the weight of her breasts, leashed into a suntop that seems to have been made out of yellow towelling, hunches her forward and he finds himself looking right into her eyes.

"You take care." She reaches out with blunted fingers and touches him on the arm. The hands of women have touched him more in the last few weeks than in the last twenty years. Ministering hands. "Remember that I've been a nurse and, once a nurse, always." She laughs and withdraws her fingers, almost shyly. "No one can play the old pieces like you, Jack. I've always looked forward to coming to Grace Lake just to hear you in the evenings."

In the evening by the moonlight
You can hear. . . .

He pauses along the sandpath to North Cabin, bracing a hand against a birch with ravaged bark. Kids never leave it alone, always tearing, peeling. It's a wonder the tree is still alive. Waves of dizziness pass over him. The heat. Sitting for so long. Moisture runs onto his glasses from his forehead. A clean handkerchief: Mrs. Washburne has ironed it into a neatly-folded square. He cleans the lenses first, testing them against the afternoon sun. Then the perspiration along his face. Clean, dry vision.

The lake is perfectly still and the islands close to the east edge scrape the unclouded blue and rest in their mirror images. Red-winged blackbirds move lazily from cattail clump to cattail clump, last year's dead stalks and convoluted leaves, this year's new green thrusting. Epaulets of blood. Is there a legend about that, the wounded wings, flight in pain? There is strawberry blight along the path like more blood, clotted onto green stalks. Crush them and make red ink, they cried as children, with the red oozing against their fingers. Lipstick, shrieked Olga Karpinski, rubbing it on her mouth. Or was it Helen Burch? The teacher made her stay in and write lines. She didn't see where Orest Polchek had rubbed his red ink though, showing off to all the playground the wonder of his sex emerging from the unbuttoned opening of his trousers like some strange scarlet animal, querulous, quivering. When he got home he had hurried down to the lake and its screen of willows and tried it on himself, rubbing the red juice against his small hardness until he hurt but it was nothing like Orest had to show and he woke up in the night, sore and crying. Hush my baby, his mother crooning, and he could feel her breast through her nightgown, full and soft. Mama's here, mama's here. You just tell her about that bad old nightmare. But he couldn't tell.

The dizziness ebbs further away and his feet can move again. In North Cabin the air is close, hot and stale. Someone has cleaned the winter out of it. Brown wool has been stretched taut over his bunk. Mrs. Steinhauer or Adeline must have made it up. Winter frost or else a leak in the ceiling has made watery inroads into the mural that a redheaded boy, Albert Garner—Gardener?—painted last summer. The sky seeps into the mountains, trees and lake run in aquamarine rivulets along the bone-coloured calcimine to the floor. There is a brown smudge that was once a deer.

On his worktable, someone—Adeline?—has left a bouquet of tiger lilies in a sealer jar. Next to his cot, the curtains from the farmhouse, his mother's parlour curtains, have been restrung as a partition. They still seem oddly displaced. River-green with metallic threads worked through them, they had always framed the small, hopeless orchard. Silver threads among the green.

He falls asleep on the shank of the afternoon, the door propped open with a rock, a slight breeze coming in from the lake, brushed with the sounds of small birds, the insistent droning of a fly, the intermittent rustling of poplar leaves.

It is not an easy sleep in the heat and he becomes caught up in a dream that is insistent and fretful. His mother is coming up to the house past the barren fruit trees, heavy as she was in those last couple of years, breathing with difficulty. Jackie, she's calling with some urgency. Jack, are you there? He hides behind the green curtains. There are small china figurines on the window ledge, miniatures set side by side with their own peculiar distortions: a blue jay larger than a horse, a ballerina with one arm extended to the tip of a squirrel's tail. If he moves them, his mother will set them back exactly as they were, in their places. Jack? she calls, coming through the door. The voice tentative, almost crying. I know you're there. He can smell the curtains. Dust and a memory of his father's pipe tobacco. A glint of silver thread. He turns his head and, through the window glass, he can see the trees, the road leading down to the lake and, farther away, waves of fields edged with trees. Beyond them, three miles away, he can make out the tallest buildings in the small town where he goes to school and his mother gives piano lessons: two grain elevators and one church spire. It is the edge of the world. He remains still, frozen between transparencies, the glass with its knowledge of the universe, the curtains folded against the small parlour, the close furniture.

"Jack?"

His eyes are open. Dusk softens the definition of the table, the cots, the curtain edge. There is enough light yet to yield the lilies a soft orange, fading red, candle yellow.

"Jack?" The woman in the doorway is heavy like his mother, but a larger presence. "We saved you a bite of supper. You were sleeping so sound." The voice is Adeline Tupper's; the bulk settles into the familiarity of her form. It is a struggle to get up, to find balance and move across the room to the door. Her hand flutters out as if to assist and then retreats as his feet move more steadily.

At one end of the mess hall a trestle table has been covered with a cloth and there are wildflowers in another sealer jar as a centrepiece. Lilies and lungwort and bladder campion. A sprig of red-petalled windflowers.

"The lilies," he remembers. "Thank you, Adeline."

"All set to take the Nature Day trophy again?" she laughs. "North Cabin never gives anyone else a chance."

"It's a fair contest." In front of him is the saved chop covered with congealing mushroom-soup sauce, limp string beans, salad greens in a slick of oil. Mrs. Steinhauer beams at him, brandishing an egg turner.

"I have to warn you, there's a challenge in my rocks." Frank Tupper is into a dish of tapioca pudding, probably not his first of the evening. "I've been studying up this past winter."

He tries not to think of the chop and swallows a bite unchewed. It settles in his throat. The tea is lukewarm, heavy with steeping.

"I'm afraid I'm not very hungry."

"Try some of Millie's tapioca." Tupper allows the concluding spoonful from his pudding dish to make its own statement, quivering, gelatinous, like frog spawn gone to mouth.

"I wonder if the piano is as out of tune as I think it probably is?" He moves to it, lifts the key protector, tries the yellowing middle C. Closer than one would expect. His fingers explore an arpeggio. Better than eating.

He plays for an hour until the pain settles high across his back. Adeline's quavering soprano moves eagerly into the songs. *Hope with a gentle persuasion.* Bragge and Tupper and McEvoy make a stab at barbershop harmony. *One leaf is sunshine, the second is rain; third is the roses.* He plays variations on *Glow Worm* and then settles into *Liebestraum.* With a third of the notes slightly off key, the piece has a feel of decay to it. *My dream of love was meant to live forever.* Odd words, courting the inertia of the dream rather than the hope of realization. He can't remember the German words. Perhaps they are something entirely different. The singers have drifted back to the table, except for Adeline who seems to take pleasure from contact with the piano itself. *O Adeline, sweet Adeline.* Chopin's *Tristesse Etude* is for her. She smiles, pleased that he has remembered her favourite, and squeezes his shoulder when he has finished.

"How about *Elise*?" Shirley Stickles has come back to stand by Adeline. "I love *Für Elise.*"

"If you've heard it murdered every second day for thirty years you might develop a different feeling for it." He flexes his fingers.

"Oh, really," she giggles. "That would be painful."

But he finishes with it, beginning so softly that there is only the suggestion of sound, and then building definition. You have the facility, Dr. Woerkum had told him just before graduation, to appear to be discovering a piece for the first time whenever you play it. Don't ever lose that. Malcolm had overheard and when they were back in the dorm he was choking with laughter.

Come on. That was a compliment. Why are you laughing?

Oh, I dunno. It just struck me as funny. Always the first time. You're like a virgin with an endless supply of cherries.

You pig.

"Bravo." Shirley Stickles leads the clapping, a noise echoing now into the night, startling the loons far out on the lake. For a minute there is only the sound of their ululating lament against the night's lateness.

"I think I'd better call it a day."

Mrs. Steinhauer has wrapped biscuits in a tea towel for him. It is darkening along the sandpath to North Cabin. He will turn on the lantern. Press the elephant ear under "E" in his grandfather's dictionary. Read until sleep. It may come quickly.

THREE

He wakes early, lurching suddenly into the soft-edged warmth of the morning, his blankets on the floor, his pyjamas soaked with sweat. It is an hour, he realizes, before Mrs. Steinhauer will have the coffee on. Removing his damp pyjamas, he hangs them over the cord holding up the green curtains. His body looks yellow in the muted morning light, his skin the skin of cream left uncovered, waxy and smooth in places, wattled and hanging where he has lost the most weight along his upper arms and legs. Somewhere in his grip, Mrs. Washburne has folded his swimming shorts. You need a new pair, she informed him. These have seen enough ups and downs. They have those nylon stretch kind on sale at McIntosh's. It was true; he did need a new pair, but he felt a reluctance to give up the ones he had worn for so many years. Didn't actors often have a special pair of shoes or a hat that they wore out of superstition? He felt something the same for his old swim shorts. Malcolm would have died laughing over that. Would have had some smart thing to say, or some crazy variation on a song. *Pack up your penis in your old swim suit and smile, smile, smile.*

If it is possible, today will be even hotter than yesterday. The mist is already burning off the far shore. Someone is into the lake before him, splashing, leaping and plunging like a dolphin, flashing red trunks. The young swimming instructor, bronzed and blonde. In the nylon stretch kind. He bobs up and down, spitting water, laughing and waving.

"Come on in. The water's perfect."

The beach is good this year, the water level down enough to expose sand. He leaves the soap and towel on the grass skirting the sand and wades in, the tepid water meeting his advance, encircling, soothing. Hydrotherapy. Is that what it's called? Like a child who has not yet learned to swim, he is lying down, just his head out, the palms of his hands flat on the sandbottom. His body is floating, soft, white now like the under-belly of a beached pike, moving ever so slightly with the undulations of the lake. Even when it is still, there is movement, a force within the water. A kind of seduction really, to lie suspended, inert, drifting. All he has to do is lift his hands from the lakebottom.

Shirley Stickles and Adeline Tupper have appeared, picking their way gingerly past thistles. "Yoohoo," Adeline trills and McEvoy scampers toward them in great splashes, setting currents into motion. He runs circles around them, laughing and shaking water off himself like a spaniel as they shriek at him and pelt him with sand.

"Be on our side, Jack," Adeline screams, but before he can respond they have raced past him into deeper water. He watches the sand settle back onto the rippled surface of the bottom. The laughter and shouting seem to come from a great distance but there is a comfort in it, a kind of buoyancy like the water itself. He drifts, eyes closed, until the swimmers scramble up through the sand and grass toward their cabins.

For the first time in many weeks, he has developed an appetite, putting away three of Mrs. Steinhauer's flapjacks. Breakfast will not be so casual once the boys have arrived. They linger over second cups of coffee. Discussion has drifted to Drama Night plans.

"I'll help the boys with props and costumes." Shirley Stickles is flushed with enthusiasm, her hands busy with her glasses, her hair, a shell necklace on her t-shirt. "It can go in their craft time. We'll do it all together."

A Drama Night centred around Bible stories. Whose idea is that? Skits from the good book. The boys will be outraged, he knows. His years at the camp have given him an instinct for reckoning their grievances. Nature Day, his domain, comes with its own territory of complaints. Time has been an ally, though. Nature projects have been part of the Grace Lake activity schedule for summers beyond the recall of even the most faithful campers among the boys. He has shored the ritual with a small storeroom stocked with Bristol board and display frames, bottles of formaldehyde, prepared tempera and India ink. The trophy, sporting an etched frieze of plants and animals, has added a sense of permanency, its base crusted with small shields dominated by North Cabin winners. He has perfected the project over the years, moving from mixed teams to cabins choosing their own themes. Birds. Small animals. Rocks: Reverend Tupper for that one. Flowers. North Cabin, as always, will work with flowers. Two years ago, a boy had created a gigantic poster of a tiger covered with pressed tiger lilies, the stripes and features worked in with India ink, Blake's poem, *Tyger, tyger, burning bright*, lettered at its base.

The boy's name is gone but the image is there, suddenly clear and immediate, the bent head, thin hands gluing fragile petals within the black outline of the beast. Flushed with his achievement, the boy had let him keep the poster and he had taken it back to town and put it in his study until the petals crumbled and flaked away except where daubs of glue held the tattered remnants. He let Mrs. Washburne complain for three weeks before he finally discarded it. Bleedin' tiger, he had heard her muttering. A body's got better thing's to do than cleaning up tiger dust.

A car has driven up. There is sudden quiet at the table. The sound of a door slamming is followed by a piping voice: "I wanna stay too. Howcome Stanley gets to. . . . "

"To your stations, troops," Tupper laughs.

They refuse to let him help with registration, though, protesting good-naturedly. When he leaves them, he heads back to North Cabin but walks past it to the edge of the camp lot where the bush is thick and the plant growth is heavy, almost jungle-like to the height of an adult's knee. It is not a conscious decision to walk along the farm road leading back from the campsite and he is at the first of a series of three gates before he realizes where he is headed. Of course, he has always made this walk, at least once each summer, even the summer after he brought Roy Dejarlais to camp. Why do you want to go back there, Reverend Smight had asked him, using his voice of the protector, the building contractor checking on hard hats. He has no memory of what he answered, only a memory of the compulsion, the determination to go alone, to survey the mossy hummocks, the stagnant water, the marsh grass. After a few summers, the swamp changed, sinking in some places, pushing forth new growth in others, the water shifting, so that it became impossible to say the boy lay there, this is where we found him, this is where Smight, after hefting him into his arms, nearly fell.

Off into the dormant fields, tiger lilies scatter like tongues of prairie fire. The roses this year are pale, almost white. One of his mother's water-colours comes to mind, wild roses spilling out of a yellow china vase. You get your love of flowers from me, Jackie, she said, and that's the truth. He can see her at the piano, her fingers caressing the keys, her voice lost in an old song. *There's a rose that grows in no man's land.*

Back from the road, flanking the fields, the muskeg will have its own flowers. Sometimes there are cloudberries, white, crepey petals against crimped leaves, almost hidden in the sphagnum moss. Roy Dejarlais discovered some the first day of camp; they had walked along this road together and the boy kept running off into the bush, returning every few minutes with some botanical treasure or other. He knew his way around a swamp.

It takes him longer than usual to walk to the dead poplar at the edge of the fallow fields where a confusion of growth runs against barbed wire and the order of an oat crop. There are tangles of vetch and alfalfa, purple and pinkish-blue, some stinkweed (his mother used to call it penny cress) and tansy mustard. He sits down, leaning against the tree, waiting for his breath to ease, to regulate. Generally he has cut through the brush going back. Unlike the road, it has changed from summer to summer. One spot, a slough, has dried up completely. A balm tree, a beacon the boys always called "The Big Tree," was struck by lightning two years ago. Riven down the middle and seered with fire. He would like to see what has happened to it, whether it held to life or gave itself over to ants and fungus. But it will take all the energy he has to retrace his steps to the compound. His feet do not want to leave the road, the smooth, baked ruts.

Two of the North Cabin campers are there when he gets back. He checks off their names on the first sheet on the clipboard. "James Potherby." He reads it aloud.

"Jimmy."

The boy, frail and freckled, wears the new style of metal-rimmed glasses, a faded hockey sweater, faded jeans and sneakers.

"Any cot, Jimmy. First come. . . . " He nods to the other boy, standing like a pylon in the middle of his gear. "Wayne Bowmeister. Let me see, were you at camp last year?"

"Yeah. South Cabin, but I had you in Bible Study."

"Ah." He remembers him. A slow, smiling, shuffling boy with bad teeth and hair poorly cut, always in need of combing. He has grown a lot since last summer. A boy anxious to please, he brought him stalks of water parsnip when he was supposed to be logging water birds for Tupper's Nature Day team. Once they have decided on their cots and he has answered their questions, he leaves them alone to get settled and walks to the beach. The camp is beginning to stir with sound, the calls of boys, the yapping of a dog, the idling of motors. Heys, hellos, farewells. It is a different place now. There is a humming, a force like the surge of lake water. From the dock he can see that another two figures have gone into North Cabin.

When he goes back up to the cabin and checks their names off on the register, he remembers them from last summer. Mike Mac-Donald and Clayton Burgess. They are both friendly, boisterous. Burgess's face has blossomed with acne. The thick, laughing lips, he recalls, can quickly turn sullen.

"Hey, Mr. Hislop, you still North Cabin? Still finding flowers? Is Mr. Tupper still camp director?" MacDonald doesn't wait for any answers. He is busy flicking Burgess with his towel. "Boy, am I ever hot and sticky."

Burgess grabs the towel. They are both big for their age, looking eighteen rather than sixteen. "I hope the Girl Guides are over at the Point Camp again this year." He tosses the towel up, catches it on his index finger. "Maybe we can get together for a dance night. Remember last year—"

"Mike. Clayton." He startles them by shaking their hands. It is an effort, the reaching out, the acceptance of the smooth-skinned hands, the contact of his fingers against their fingers. Somehow the act reduces them. MacDonald is suddenly all awkward moves, running his hand through his hair as if to loosen the tight curls, running his tongue back and forth over his lips. Burgess flushes; his acne shines. Averted eyes wander over the cabin, the rows of cots, the slung curtain, the two younger boys. Introductions are made with the same formality as the shaking of hands. Bowmeister and Potherby acknowledge with a duck of their heads.

"Who else we got bunking?" Burgess, tired of the towel, has flopped onto a cot. "Christ, I hope not Pissin' Parker. It's like sleeping next to a toilet."

"Language, Burgess." Their eyes lock for a minute and then Burgess looks away. "I might as well tell you right now there will be a demerit system in effect."

MacDonald laughs. "Sure thing, Mr. Hislop. Any of these guys swear, I'll wash their mouths out with Lifebuoy for you. You hear that, Clayboy?"

"Ah shut up, faggot." Looking for a reaction. "Faggot ain't swearing. It's like a piece of firewood."

"Hey, you going to let him call me firewood, Mr. Hislop? Can I have permission to break his legs?"

The bell at the hall clangs a tinny

announcement of lunch.

"Is Steinhauer back cooking?" Burgess admires the neat line of his bed roll. "Maybe they want to see if she can actually kill someone off this year."

"You new?" MacDonald pokes Potherby. "If they're serving chili, don't eat it. Deadly stuff. I had the trots for a month."

The door slams. Voices fade. His breakfast still seems heavy in his stomach and he eases himself onto his cot. A rest is what he needs, not lunch. On the orange crate serving as a make-shift bookshelf and bed-table, there is his grandfather's dictionary with its brown covers, cracking with age. Always his pressing book. When had he thought of placing them under their initial letters? C for crocus. T for toadflax. E for elephant head. Delicate and two-dimensional. Waiting to be glued in his album. *Albumblatt. Tee-duh-duh-duh-duh-dah-DUH-dah-dum. Album-blatt für Elise.* How many thousands of times has he heard the conjunction of notes and yet never quite the same? The boys too, never quite the same. Shy, frightened, brash, wearing their colours. MacDonald and Burgess trying to appear tough. It will take energy—and sleep. The red darkness of closed eyelids. Last night's pain across his shoulders has suffused and lies less insistently across his chest. You just have a wee lie-down and let me close these shades. Mrs. Washburne is all for filtered light. Let me tilt the venetians so it's soft lighting. There now. His

mother's words: there now. A benediction. The
doctor says complete bed-rest. He wants to get
down off the Winnipeg couch. You can just pee
into the chamber pail and we'll put the lid back
on. That's the good thing about having one with a
lid. No need to leave the couch. Just off for a
minute and then back up. You don't want to spoil
your heart. She is gone. He gets up, his bare feet
on the cold linoleum of the living room. She calls
it a parlour. His hands against the green curtains, the silver threads. She is walking through
the orchard, fat, anxious, distraught.

He hides behind the curtains. She is at the
door, breathless, crying. How can she know that
he has been to the lake by himself? If he is very
still, maybe she will go and do something and forget about him. But where are his clothes? He will
need to go back to the lake. They must be there.
Hey, someone calls. He looks out the window and
there is Malcolm waving his green corduroy
jacket. Malcolm!

"Hey, Chief! He was in my cabin last year."
Burgess's voice? "Good timing. You missed lunch.
Dog shit on toast."

Someone has pulled the curtains so that they
extend along the length of his cot, making his bed
corner hot and dark. He is damp with perspiration again. Beyond the edge of the curtain, he can
see the sealer of flowers, the metal piping of the
nearest cot.

Chief?

"Don't talk loud. Hislop's asleep." The voice, shifting registers, sounds like MacDonald's.

"Oh Christ. Not Hislop." Whispering. "Don't tell me we've got Hislop. Maybe we could complain."

"Complain to old man Tupper? Forget it. Garry Cheshire complained last year and ended up peeling spuds for three fucking days. Besides, Hislop ain't so bad. You just got to watch that you don't say Jesus Christ or fuck around him." Thank you, Clayton Burgess. "You balled any girls yet?" Silence.

"Uh—sure. Lots." Potherby's voice, tremulous.

"Lots?"

"Yeah? Like how many? Three? Sixteen? Two hundred?"

"The Chief did last year." MacDonald interrupting, his voice just above a whisper. "Remember you told me about it, Cardinal. The Girl Guide with the big knockers. Kee-rist. Four times in two hours. You could hardly walk for two days."

Cardinal.

"Probably sore from jerking off." Burgess scoffing.

There is a pause in the chatter. The sound of the screen door being eased closed.

"Hey, Travis!" A slow, near-drawl. Not Burgess or MacDonald. Cardinal? "This here's Travis

Carroway. I rode down on the bus with him. This guy's got a record-player and a whole suitcase full of records. Good stuff too."

"You think Hislop's going to let us play records?"

"Don't we get free time?"

He should get up. How long has he slept? Without his glasses, the watch dial is blurred. Where are his glasses? On top of the dictionary? The craziness of dreams. Malcolm had never even been to the acreage and yet the mind can place him on the path through the orchard, up from the lake, put in his hand that old corduroy jacket he hadn't worn since he was twelve.

"We got Hislop." MacDonald has lowered his voice as close as he can to a whisper. "Now, young gentlemen," an affected, mincing tone, "no improper language, and everybody say their prayers, and no jacking off. You hear?"

"He's gotta sleep sometime." Cardinal's slow musing. "Then I'm heading for the Point Camp."

"You like to do it to little boys?" Bowmeister's high giggle. "I heard the Scouts are there first this year."

"Fuck. My luck."

Bowmeister's head peeps around the curtains.

"What's the time, Bowmeister?"

"Uh . . . Mr. Hislop. Thought you was asleep. Anyone got the time?"

"Two ten."

"Everyone here now?"

"Two more guys. Luke Cardinal and Travis Carroway. Came down on the bus. One bunk's still empty."

Glasses. Joints stiff. Steady. Steady on his feet. Cardinal's features lock into memory from last summer. Could almost be a twin to that Dejarlais boy. White teeth against dark skin. A bit huskier.

"Hi, Mr. Hislop. This here's Travis Carroway."

The new boy is lying on his bunk. Golden. Sunbronzed skin, sunbleached hair. Different. What is it? Sandals, not running shoes. White shorts. White t-shirt. Grey eyes, unblinking, taking measure briefly before moving past him, seeking the wall, the window.

"Travis, this here's Mr. Hislop."

The boy inclines his head in a gesture that might be a nod of response before he laughs, a quiet, almost inaudible laugh.

FOUR

In the free time following lunch on the second day of camp, John Hislop finds himself walking from building to building, his large hands moving over the wood, touching the door frame of a granary that they converted into the first cabin, touching the board sheeting of the south cabin, the last they built, already warped and weathered and needing repair. It felt good, he remembers, to work with the hammer and the saw. He and Smight had done a good deal of the work over a period of three summers. Not a bad job for amateurs, although Smight had considered himself a professional. The minister glowing with the joy of the labour, the joy of literally working into his favourite metaphor. The ecstasies of work and faith. That young counsellor had shone with them too. The evening on the island, as the campers slept, he talked about personal revelation. The call of God like a surge of electricity turning impotent steel to a powerful tool. The young man savouring his figure of speech. Plugging in to prayer. His hands had grown active with the excitement of his message, the withered hand fluttering against his chest. With his good hand he had reached over and clasped his wrist. There are times when he can feel the hand, the current of life along the fingers, moving against his own blood.

Supper is impossible to eat. He nibbles on a piece of dry bread, sips some tea, and then excuses himself. He does not mean to fall asleep in the lounge chair, but when he does, it is as if the dream is waiting for him. He walks down through the orchard to the small lake that lapped against one corner of the acreage. It has a name, Ferble's Lake, but he has always called it Mirror Lake. Mrs. Carey is standing, poised at the lake's edge, and as he comes closer he can see the Indian boy, it must be Roy Dejarlais, lying on the bank, naked except for his undershorts. This isn't the place for him, she says, her bright bird-eyes sharp with a kind of knowledge. He should be placed up in the branches, closer to the sky. She is right, of course, that would be the proper place for the boy's body, but aspen branches are not made for such burdens. The grass must do for now. It is softened by its nearness to the slough, softened and cropped by animals. Use this to clean him, she says, pulling a cloth out of her purse. It is something crocheted, maybe an antimacasser. He brushes a smudge of dirt from the face, smooths the hair, damp curls against the ear, against the neck, against the forehead skin stretched and taut. He can hear his mother calling, this time from up the hill, from the direction of the house. His name, over and over again. Her voice anxious and distraught, coming nearer. He tries to call out, No, go back, but no sound will come out of his mouth, his throat, until finally there is one strangled howl.

"Are you okay?"

A woman is in the doorway. Aproned, rag in hand, the cloth dripping on the plywood floor. A small artery has trickled to his right foot. The chair is soft. Are the hands on the worn green cloth of the arms his own? They rest so still, so distant, but there is the feeling of fluted wood against his fingertips. Along the floor the water trickles to his left foot.

"I thought I heard someone holler."

The room holds smells of dust and disinfectant and trapped heat. Faintly, Jesus lifts his lantern. The generations sleep. The woman is Mrs. Steinhauer.

"What time is it?"

"It's nearly eight-thirty." Her eyebrows are puckered with worry. She shifts the dripping rag abstractedly to her other hand.

"I must have fallen asleep." With effort his right foot shifts, then his left. The power in his fingers is not gone. He can make his body rise. "Where is everyone?"

"Mostly all down at the bonfire. I saved you some supper. You got to eat more." She dries the ragless hand against the bulge of her stomach. Spaghetti, he remembers.

The bonfire has been delayed until the dusk settles into a more fire-defining darkness. A soccer ball moves erratically along the grass of the bank, boys running, scattering, drawing together along its path. In the fire pit, the wood has been laid, layer by diminishing layer, to build a tower. The strange boy, the silent, laughing, golden boy still in white shorts adds a wooden crate to the top. A step-tower built by jungle Indians, standing tiptoe in feathers and blood, to reach a little higher into heaven.

The last boy is there, stirring ashes at the tower base with a willow stick, a fat, distracted boy who arrived in the middle of supper, waddling down the central aisle between the tables, creating a breeze of titters, laughter choked with spaghetti. The savagery of edge-eyed looks. Wesley something. Made him think of the fat boy he and Malcolm had seen at the Edmonton Exhibition, boy or man? It was hard to tell. A Fatty

Arbuckle face, except for the blonde tufts of hair. Naked arms held up to show the soft, hanging folds of flesh. Stomach spilling out over satin-cased thighs. There was the smell of sawdust and sweat and the sound of a carousel wheezing *The Man on the Flying Trapeze.*

Terry McEvoy has a guitar and strums through a series of chords devoid of sharps or flats. *The daring young man.* Evening moves onto the lake and is carried by the loons to the rush-thick islands, the darkening pines. Adeline Tupper lifts her head from her book, rubs her eyes, pulls a sweater over her shoulders, tries to stretch it across her breasts. Shirley Stickles sits beside her with a sketchpad and a piece of charcoal, smudging the view. Barefoot boys run in and out of the water with small bark boats. Two are building a sand city. Others sprawl on the grass or sit dangle-legged on the dock.

A hand on his shoulder.

"Marvelous night for a campfire." Frank Tupper speaks as if in confidence. "We should have a riproaring one. That Carroway kid organized it all. Had a work team sorting the wood by length if you can believe it. Maybe we should put him in charge of the duty roster. He'd probably have them all begging to peel potatoes." Greying stubble along the chin. Square fingers caressing the silver whistle, shoelace-strung, resting like an amulet on his barrel chest. He brings it to mouth. The whistle's shrillness pierces the soft dark, startling birds, stirring leaves, sending ripples through the noise of the boys playing. There is a surge of sound and then quiet.

"Okay," the minister's voice booms against cabin wall and child chest and rings out over the lake. "Time to light the bonfire. Where's Carroway?"

The boy in the white shorts appears, white cloth, gold skin, cornsilk hair muted by the dusk, but the richness almost tangible.

"This is Carroway's masterpiece," Tupper continues shouting, "so he gets to set the torch." The square fingers proffer matches. Faces and figures rank around the fire pit. Sand is brushed from a naked haunch, lifted foot. The boy kneels, strikes the match, and sets it against crumpled paper leading into the bottom layer of the pyramid. Flames flicker inwardly toward the top to cheers and applause, Tupper's voice rising over all, like smoke.

Jimmy Potherby and Wayne Bowmeister have moved up silently beside him. They regard the growing fire with solemn eyes. Cardinal is standing with a comradely arm across Carroway's shoulder. The flames yield the whiteness, the gold, confirm the half smile.

"*On top of Old Smoky*," the guitar-player's voice gathers strength and catches other voices as it moves into the song. One of them a clear, true soprano. Wesley, his willow wand held still. Someone with a new man's voice cracking on *snow*. A ripple of laughter. Adeline Tupper being careful not to overpower the boys. *I lost my true lover.* . . . Another voice. Whose? A sweet tenor, caressing the words, a voice for lamplight and oiled pews, a voice to hold the soft cushion of an organ's sonority. Whose? A small explosion, sap gone to fire, sparks hurled out of the pyramid's superstructure. On the highest notes his eyes close: Malcolm. Yes, Malcolm. Oh God. The sparks die before they get very high. That one night he carried Gounod's *Ave Maria* to the plaster cupids and the varnished beams of the conservatory-hall ceiling and then came back and drew five hundred eyes into his own. Grey eyes lit with hanging lamplight. *The hours I spent with thee, dear heart.* Was that the encore? Never able to sleep after a performance. Moving around the room in his bathrobe like Joseph's coat, moonlight from the window giving his neck, his smooth face, the whiteness of polished bone, giving his auburn hair a softer shade of gold. *For a false-hearted lover.* . . .

They are doing the song again, this time Frank Tupper speaking each line so that the singing comes in an echo. The voice again from behind Adeline Tupper. Could it be Burgess? Or maybe Cardinal? It was *The Rosary* he sang. And sat up until three, smoking, the end of his cigarette glowing in the grey, moonlit room. Talking between long pauses because of course he knew sleep wasn't there for either of them. The plans. They had thought of getting a small band together. It's got to be better than giving voice lessons and playing the organ in some hick town. Choir practice on Wednesday nights. With you on piano and me on bass— I could do bass if I really got down to work— all we'd really need is someone on sax and someone on guitar. Had any of it turned out the way he wished it would have? *For a false-hearted lover, will lead you to the grave.*

Cheering. The pyramid burning bright. Mac-Donald and Burgess off by themselves singing sotto voce. *On top of spaghetti, all covered with shit. . . .*

The whistle blows.

"I wish I was a little bar of soap," Tupper proclaims to the lake, to the trees, the clear, deepening sky, his flock. There is a lone boy on the dock with an ember in his hands. White shorts, moongold hair. He moves the ember to his mouth. Smoke suffuses the contours of his face. Cigarettes are out. I don't mean cutting down; I mean totally out. Kaput. Finis. More words, doled out like pills, from Dr. Grodey. Even the second-hand smoke of the Legion won't be good for you. But I don't want you back there anyway until I give you a clean bill. He had played there regularly since the war ended and the Churchill Lounge was built, spilling out from one side of the Legion Hall. The town magistrate donated the piano on which his son had spent hundreds of talentless hours before going overseas to let his blood seep into the saltwashed sand of a Normandy beach. That *Berkeley Square*, Mrs. Washburne's voice cutting through the lounge

hubbub, that's my favourite song of all time. Always one to sing along, her warble cuts into the hall smoke, the toilet smell, the oiled babble of the lounge. Bowers of kleenex flowers loop down to the sound. Grahamc Washburne belches and pounds his chest. Kee-rist. *Roll Me Over in the Clover.* How about that one? Old soldiers never die. His fingers move along the familiar, hesitating notes of *That certain night . . . that night we met . . . there was magic abroad in the air.*

The whistle blows. *A nightingale sang. . . .*

"Boom, boom, ain't it great to be crazy?"

"Yeah," the smaller boys chorus.

Mrs. Carey had been crazy. His mother said if she'd been worsc thcy would have sent her off to Ponoka. But who was hurt if she walkcd naked along the summer road with saskatoon blossoms in her hair, her shockwhite hair, her greying bush. Your Jackie likes flowers, she told his mother on one of her visits, so I brung him these larkspurs. The craziness dormant in her eyes watching him on his bed. My little boy had rheumatic fever too. And then she sat and cried into her tea and he took a sprig of larkspur and pressed it under "L" and turned to see if the tiger lily had dried and flattened under "T". The doctor says complete bedrest and he'll be okay. There's always worry about ruining the heart, you know. His mother put the remaining sprigs in her yellow vase. He could tell by the look in her eye that she was already seeing them as a watercolour.

A horse and a flea and three blind mice sat on a tombstone shooting dice. The song has taken on the sound of a chant.

Flames are licking the crated tower, orange tongues of the night. The fat boy's face is red from his nearness. Adeline Tupper eases her sweater back off the green spill of her breasts. When there is a moment of quiet, her voice soars with the sparks into *Ezekial saw a wheel a-rollin 'way in the middle of the sky.* The sky is dark now, the wheel of the moon white gold, the stars spinning. They sing *Jacob's Ladder* and *Swing Low, Sweet Chariot* and Terry McEvoy puts away the guitar and tells the first ghost story, his voice settling softly, hypnotically, as the fire burns down and the marshmallows come out. It ends with him shouting, "Give me my bone!" which startles Shirley Stickles, making her drop her marshmallow in the fire.

"I'd like to give her my bone." He can hear MacDonald whispering to Burgess.

Burgess grunts.

Carroway has come back up from the dock, standing across from him, watching him. The grey eyes look sly, feral in the dying firelight. His smile seems to be tipped with some special meaning. He moves a white marshmallow to his mouth.

"Hey, Carroway, you're supposed to fry 'em first," Cardinal yells. The boy shrugs and laughs, the barely audible laugh, and shows his hands.

Empty.

"Use my stick," says Wesley.

Carroway smiles at him. "Roast one for me, okay?"

Tupper and Bragge come down the hill from the hall bearing a boiler of cocoa as if it were the ark of the covenant. Mrs. Steinhauer follows, laden with cups. One of the small boys is crying, the fretful weeping of a too-tired child. Adeline Tupper pulls him onto her lap as he used to like to sit, his head against his mother's breast, her arms cradling him, crooning. *If that mockin' bird don't sing* . . . Two boys have stuck the ends of their marshmallow sticks into the burning coals until they glow and are whirling them against the dark. Wheels within wheels a-glowin', frail circles of fire that the eye inscribes. Someone makes them stop. The whistle-blower, shrieking his sound against the now full night, the starlit darkness.

"Join hands and make a circle." Potherby's hand is lost in his left, the guitar-player's friendly and certain in his right. There is only the slightest glow from the coals, the reduced pyramid. Across the circle its builder has joined hands with Cardinal and Wesley. His whiteness, his goldness draws lights from the embers and he stands, a quiet angel, softly irridescent, alien.

Day is done. . . . The sweet tenor voice rising. It must be Cardinal.

Gone the sun

From the lake. . . .

It lies black and deep, the lake, mirroring the odd pinpoint of a star. The force of water, life, surging. Something there that trickles past time itself like the yearning of the seas for the moon. *From the sky. . . .* Deep and dark. That summer Roy Dejarlais died, the lake swallowed two children, teenagers really. Were they twins? They were found clinging together, as one, their eyes open as if they had drowned watching the underwater's advance, the undulating plants, the nibbling pike, the water worms. Their father came in an old pickup truck to the Grace Camp shore where they were finally discovered. Wrapped them in canvas in the truck's back, closed their eyes.

God is nigh.

FIVE

Often at the Grace Lake camp there are spells of
heat capped with thunderstorms, but his last
summer there John Hislop makes a note of the
days that follow one another without the relief of
rain, each day the heat intensifying, the humidity
increasing so that the air becomes heavy and
damp, too still to move. Even the birds grow
lethargic and quiet. For several days a red-winged
blackbird, head cocked, eye primeval and knowing, watches him, as the words of the scripture
lessons spill over the children in the Bible study
group. The youngest before him, crosslegged on

the grass, holding the miracles, the fishes, the loaves, the dying child cured. *Tell me the stories of Jesus, I love to hear.* Their voices are small and reedlike. Words of the miracles, like notes in piano pieces. Can he say them as if he were saying them for the first time?

One day he tells them the story of Noah, of the water prevailing exceedingly upon the earth, the words feeling cool in his mouth. But his thoughts are not with Noah, not with the male and female of all flesh. The breath of life is not in his nostrils; he drifts through the water, over the sunken cities, the water-bloated herds, touches the hand of the dead shepherd boy. From a distance he hears the children naming the animals they would take, male and female, onto the sanctified vessel.

By the time he has dismissed them and sent them scattering back to their cabins, his own boys have returned from their lesson with Reverend Tupper. Cigarette smoke hangs in the motionless cabin air despite MacDonald's efforts to fan it away with his hands. The cigarettes have disappeared, except for Carroway's. He cups it inside his palm and smiles and stares through him, stares at the ruined mural, seems to move into it.

"Carroway," Cardinal hisses.

"I want them all." With his glasses off for a moment, he massages the bridge of his nose and places his Bible on the table. Lily petals have started to fall.

"What?"

"The cigarettes. All of them on the table here. Now." He can hear the weariness in his voice.

"I don't got any," laughs Cardinal. "Honest Injun."

The others echo his laughter.

"Search me," says MacDonald. He is sitting on his bunk, naked, about to change into his trunks, and lifts his penis away from his cushioning balls as if there would be the first place to look.

Potherby breaks into hysterical laughter. He holds his hand over his mouth, sputters, chokes; the tears stream down his face.

"Open all your grips. I want them on your bunks."

"Oh, Christ," Burgess moans.

"That's one demerit, Burgess. Five and you have the privilege of washing the dining hall floor."

"Remember, I had to do that last year." MacDonald squeezes into trunks a size too small, makes a show of getting his genitals in place. "Chri— gee whiz. These are strangling me. Told my old lady I needed a new pair." Potherby gasps for air.

Suitcases and duffel bags are lugged onto the beds.

"You too, Carroway. And put out that cigarette."

The boy eases himself from his bunk, walks slowly to the door, takes a last drag and then tosses it.

"Go and pick it up. There's a garbage pail in the corner."

He laughs, low, close to a chuckle, and takes two giant steps to retrieve the butt. Holding it with one hand, he shakes a finger at it and then goosesteps back in and over to the garbage pail.

Wesley's suitcase has burst over his bed, spilling clothing crumpled into balls, comic books, towels, chocolate bars, a View-master with its white daisies of slides, and a picture of a woman with a big smile and no chin.

"That your mother, Wesley?" Burgess captures the portrait. "Jeez, I'd like to go out on a date with her."

"Gimme it." The boy looks like he's ready to cry.

Carroway's suitcase is open. Clothes neatly folded, whites, tans, grays, all belted or pocketed in place. He opens a matching, smaller case. It holds a portable record-player, records in jackets, comics, magazines, a partial carton of cigarettes.

"You should have been a customs inspector," Carroway says, handing him the carton. "You don't need to look at anybody else's. I passed them around. Like Jesus, you know. Sharing.

One for all and all for one."

"Jesus did not happen to be one of the three musketeers." He takes the opened carton.

"Father, Son, and Holy Ghost," Carroway smirks.

"The package of cigarettes that's gone?"

He eases it out from under his pillow.

"Now let's see the magazines."

"You got a search warrant?" Carroway's smile has turned into a grimace. "There's no law against reading, is there?"

There are mainly Classic Comics. *A Tale of Two Cities, The Time Machine, The Three Musketeers* sure enough. Several *Mad* magazines, the smiling idiot face. A pulpy comic entitled *The Adventures of Dick* with a Dick Tracy figure on its cover, leering at a woman in net stockings leaning against a lamp post, holding a kitten to her bulging breasts. In the balloon of language, Tracy is saying, "I like your pussy, Babe. You wanna introduce her to Dick?"

"You like comics, Mr. Hislop, I got a ton," says Bowmeister. "*G.I. Joe.* I must have fifty of them."

The first page inside restates the title, *The Adventures of Dick.* Beneath the lettering there is a huge, veined phallus with a hand wrapped around its base, women in the distance with their hands to their foreheads, fainting. He closes it quickly.

"I think you'd better leave this with me— and the cigarettes. You realize you've chalked up enough demerits to be on chore detail for the next couple of days."

Carroway shrugs his shoulders, casts his head down, folds his hands between his knees.

"I'm," searching for a word, "disappointed." If only he could sit down. Blood seems to have left his head and rushed to other parts of his body, making his fingertips tingle, his loins stir.

"Can we go for a swim?" says MacDonald. "I'm dying. Tupper made us listen for an hour all about David and Goliath and that Jonathan guy. All I could think of was that lake out there and nobody using it."

"Didn't even mention Bathsheba," says Carroway, clicking the shining metal clasps on his luggage.

"Bathsheba?" MacDonald snaps the band of his swimsuit against his taut belly.

"The woman he took in adultery. Saw her naked in the bath."

"That's in the Bible?"

"You can all have a short swim." The faintness comes in waves. The pain like an old companion. "But remember I want each of you to have your science samples by lunchtime. Get six or seven different ones. We'll identify and press them this afternoon. I'm just—" his left hand grasping the table with such force that the few remaining petals fall, leaving exposed the pistils, the pollen-burdened stamens. "I'm just going to stay back and rest for a bit."

In two minutes they are gone and the quiet surrounds him like warm water. His hand goes from the table to the edge of the curtain. Cigarettes, *The Adventures of Dick* to the night table. File them under "C" and "D"? Old Mrs. Carey kept her sugar in a piggy bank and tea in a stationery box. The oddest things in the oddest places, his mother said after a visit. She has a special name for you. Smiling. What? What?

If he lies still and thinks of the best, most peaceful time in his entire life, maybe the pain will leave. The power of positive thinking. Some people believe in it. What's there to see on the gloomy side? Mrs. Washburne pouring tea. Even in the blitz I didn't see no reason to go around looking like doom. No point to it, if you see what I mean. Not that I didn't have cause with Dad coughing blood and Grahame off in Africa and Mrs. Eden next door with her legs blown off. The same bomb that took the pantry off Mum's and Dad's. Blew it to smithereens but you know the fruitcake we was saving for Christmas was only squashed a little bit. Best cake I ever had a bite of. The best.

There must have been a best—a good and perfect time. Those few months at the conservatory, the rush of youth through halls, up and down stairways, the mingled sounds from different rooms of a violin, a piano, a waltz by

Chopin, Mozart's night music, fading, fading into
the late hours and the silence that is defined only
by Malcolm's laughter. The trouble with you,
Jack, you're too serious. He can see him laughing, the bottle of wine half empty at his bare feet.
You're too serious. What was it he had said to
that? Life is serious. We're not going to get out of
it alive. Malcolm raising the bottle, his three-in-
the-morning cigarette dangling from his other
hand. Give me one. What, a cigarette? You don't
smoke.

Maybe I'll have a good time like you.

Or is the perfect time an hour spent by Mirror
Lake, lying in the sun? A touch of wind, just
enough to move the long willow leaves.
Dragonflies moving their odd horizontal bodies
through the air. Some mating, stately, seriously.
Others coasting on cellophane wings. A waterbug
drifting. Directly in front of his face, strawberry
plants with their tiny berries. Thinking nothing,
just lying and drifting in sun and sky and gentle
wind. Can the best time be when the world has
first given you your complete self, your complete
aloneness? The dragonflies mate. The heart stirs.
Returning pain makes new discoveries: a piece of
chest, a piece of arm, a tingle along the hand.

There is no rest. His fingers extract a
cigarette from Carroway's half-used package.
Matches? A good camper is never without. He
finds them in an empty pill bottle, secured
against dampness. A flare of sulphur, the inward
smoke, soft suffusing. The pain blurs.

He picks up *The Adventures of Dick.* Dick gets around. The streetlamp woman moaning OgodO-godOgod across the page, the kitten riding a rump. On the following page there is a bosomy nurse disrobing at a window, Dick out in the nightbushes below, gushing. Little man. His mother's name for it. You mustn't bother your little man, Jackie. Leave him be and he'll grow up pure. Floating in his bath, a small pink gumdrop. By pressing his thighs together, he can make it disappear. Only the smooth V of his groin left. The configuration of flesh makes him like his cousins Moira and Dianne.

Malcolm showering next to him, sashaying around under the water spray and singing *I'm the Sheik of Araby,* his penis standing out from its nest of red, unhooded in lather. He has named it Valentino. Unconscious of the meaning of the word embarrassment. His winterwhite body shining with soap. Water makes his hair hang in burnished ringlets against his forehead, along his groin. He moves from song to song. Barrack ballads, parodies.

> *Seated one day with my organ*
> *I was weary and ill at ease*
> *Till my fingers wandered idly. . . .*

Self-consciously, he had turned his back to him, hiding his own erection in a bath cloth. The book will need burning. Stuff it in the cookstove when Millie is away from the kitchen.

The incredible yearning. The hollowness in

his stomach, the dizziness, the rearrangement of the body's blood. What would Dr. Grodey say—a cigarette and a hard-on within twenty-four hours. Might as well have been playing piano all evening in the Churchill Lounge.

He smokes another one at the table. In for a dime. His fingers move the scattered tiger lily petals into a neat mound. He brushes the fallen pollen off the Bible, flicks ashes into the stagnant water of the sealer. Malcolm had a deadly aim with the ash end of a cigarette. He could tap ashes into the narrow opening of a wine bottle without dropping any onto the floor. How old were they when they were at the conservatory? Eighteen? Nineteen? A special breed, Malcolm. He had asked him once about the wine, the odd bottle of hooch. There's an old dame on 97th Street that'll get me anything I want, he'd laughed. The laugh that meant he was lying. By putting the sealer on the floor next to the cot, he can finish the cigarette lying down, the pillow for the moment cool against the back of his head. A rise and fall of voices echoes from the lake, sounds shared with the fury of a trapped wasp busily dying against the window.

It seems like a dream is waiting for him, almost anxiously, pressing its images against him the minute he has slipped past consciousness. Mrs. Washburne and his mother and Mrs. Carey are seated on three chairs ranked by his bed. Dr. Grodey doesn't mind, his mother speaks in a tone of forced joviality, as long as we don't tire you, so say if you're tired. Then she lowers her voice so that the others can't hear. We cleaned up the boy, washed him all over and put him in one of your shirts. You know the butcher linen that I turned the collar on. Mrs. Carey, smiling, drooling, plucking out a larkspur blossom that has been sticking in her white hair. She is humming something. *God sees the little sparrow fall.* Scarlet fever will turn into rheumatic fever faster than milk will sour in a thunderstorm, says Mrs. Washburne. I've seen it time and again. Weakens the heart if you're not careful. I think that's what the boy died from. The worst thing is the damp. My brother Tom had it in his knees when he was just a tyke. Kept him out of the war it did, so maybe it saved him after all. No, it was polio. His voice comes out as a whisper. There was polio everywhere that year. He wants to say more but his voice disappears; there is only a strangled gasping, and when he tries to get up out of the bed, he realizes he is naked. How has he become naked? How has he lost his voice? The white sheet covers. That's right. Lie back and rest. Mrs. Carey puts the larkspur blossom in her mouth. The oddest things in the oddest places. You're looking peaked, Mrs. Washburne fusses, just have one of these rhubarb tarts here. That'll perk you up. His mother is moving toward the pile of magazines to straighten them. No. He can't speak. He can't move. Maybe she won't notice it under the *Canadian Geographic*. If he could talk, he would say it must be someone else's. Just waiting to be burned. Can't let it get into the wrong hands. Don't touch it. Don't touch it. Elsie Panek comes in wearing her nurse white, her nurse smile. Visiting hours are almost up. How's our boy? How's our little man? Mrs. Washburne straightens her hat behind her pompadour, tucking a bit of stray netting into the brim. I'll just leave these tarts. His mother's hand is cool on his forehead. Time will heal, she says. Don't worry about that boy. They don't live long. But she has started to cry, her lips pulled up over her teeth, her face flesh jiggling. Soundless crying. Why? Why? Flower boy, laughs Mrs. Carey. Larkspurs are strewn on the floor around her. Water runs from one foot to the other. Oh, Mrs. Carey! They ease themselves away as hospital visitors do, with terrible smiles and a half-closed door.

He can breathe. His hands move, reaching beneath the *Canadian Geographic*. He can feel the pulpy paper and then there is the windowflash of the nurse in her little white hat with its black line. The Shebabreasts tipped with black, suckling breasts. He yearns to lay his head, yearns to brush his cheeks against the soft flesh. Fingers feel the rough-edged paper, tremble with the turning of a page. What next? The comic phallus journeying across the page, rampant, gnarled, weeping a tear. Life slipping to his centre, pooling, engorging. In the next cot a whimper, a gasping for breath. Ringlets of hair damp red-rust against the forehead, the body arching, mouth sucking in air. Furious urgency, the rhythm of bedsprings. OgodOgodOgod. The cry of death. Release. Malcolm exhaling, living again. A cigarette in the night. They need to sleep. Are there exams tomorrow? But there is music. Carnival music? The same note over and over again. A drum beating. How can anyone sleep?

He is awake, his clothes wet from sweat. A stickiness from his crotch, along his leg. He hides it with his hands. It must be Carroway's phonograph playing. There is a crescendo of drumbeats and wailing. Then silence. The screen door slamming.

"Frigging flowers." Burgess's voice. "Felt like a fucking fruitcake out there picking dandelions. Is he here?" The voice lowering to a whisper. "I stuck 'em in my shirt so no one'd see what I had. Don't see why we can't do wild animals."

Another record begins with its insistent beat of rock and roll. His suitcase is within reach. His feet touch the floor. He gets the fresh clothing ready and then peels off his shirt and puts on a clean one. Mrs. Washburne's folds stay rigid, set by the heat and the damp, along the front and the back. Into a plastic bag that she has placed with his clothing to hold garments once they need laundering, he folds the trousers, the undershorts, and towels his legs and groin quickly. The panic is less as he gets closer to finishing. The record stops.

It is past one. Carroway squats on the floor, monkeying with batteries for his phonograph.

Burgess is flat out on his cot.

"Have you had lunch?" His voice startles them. "I didn't hear the bell."

"You were sawing logs when we got back from swimming," says Burgess, "so we just went on up. Weenies and sauerkraut. Enough to make a dog puke."

Wilting clumps of flowers lie tangled on the table by his Bible, by the small mound of lily petals.

"You'll have to separate these. Press them between wax papers."

The phonograph whirrs into action again. A frenzied piano with a rock back-up, loud, straining at control, a voice filled with frantic energy, half-singing, half-shouting.

"Turn it down, Carroway."

The needle shrieks across the disc. The phonograph dies with a click, creating a silence that Burgess seems to watch with widening eyes.

"You can play it. Just not so loud."

The boy tosses his hair back from his eyes. Grey eyes, sullen, with lashes that are dark, individual, like cilia. A touch of pink surfaces along his upper cheeks. The mouth struggles for a minute before settling back to its half-smile.

"Was it worth ruining your record?"

"You can have it. Keep it with the other stuff you've taken."

Cardinal and MacDonald crash into the screen door, shouting, laughing, pummelling each other.

"Said I could beat you." Cardinal gasping.

"Beat who, asshole? You didn't beat me. It was a tie."

Burgess hissing, "Hislop's here."

Potherby, Bowmeister and Wesley trail them in.

"Stickles wants us at the craft station at two," Bowmeister announces. "We gotta decide what skit we're gonna do for Drama Night."

"Nothing's any fun this year," Burgess mutters. "Making pansy bulletin boards. Acting out stuff from the Bible."

"Remember last year, Cardinal, on Drama Night when you did the drunk Indian and that guy from West Cabin was the drunk cowboy?" MacDonald flops onto his bunk. "He was staggering around and he tripped and fell right on top of Mrs. Tupper. I thought I'd split a gut."

"Yeah. Metro." Cardinal trying to regulate his breath. "Mad-dog Metro. Told me he got a good handful of Mrs. Tupper's tit—ah, Mrs. Tupper's chest."

Potherby giggles.

"Bible skits. Wonder whose idea that was?" Burgess looking at him accusingly, the blossoms of acne reddening.

"Maybe we could do that David and

Bathsheba stuff," says Cardinal. "We could get Stickles to do the naked bathing."

"Cripes, I'd sooner look at a dog rolling in pig poop." Burgess looks at him to see if he has come close to getting a demerit.

"You'll have to work out your drama skits later." His voice has a steadiness that surprises himself. The boys are momentarily quiet. "Right now your flowers need to be sorted and pressed." He picks up one of the specimens from the table. "Whose is this one?"

"That one's mine." Wesley scuffs a sneaker along a floor board.

"Do you know what it's called?"

"I dunno. Alberta rose?"

"Well, we would like to lay claim to it but so have Iowa, North Dakota and Georgia. *Rosa acicularis* is its botanical name. Of course we know the meaning of roses in the modern floral language of romance, but back in the days of the Romans, when Jesus walked the earth, the rose was a symbol of secrecy. Its placement over the entranceway to a meeting-place meant that all who entered were bound to secrecy. This is what I expect on your charts. The common names. The botanical name. Something of the folklore."

"West Cabin is making a beaver." Burgess still muttering.

"Making a beaver!" Cardinal whoops with laughter.

"Well it beats walking in the roses with Jesus."

Carroway has retrieved his bunch of flowers from the table. The blossoms are all pale, whitish. Bog orchid. Solomon's seal. Bladder campion. He holds one sprig up to the light from the cabin window. For an instant the pale, pinkish flowers seem to invade the cabin air with their heavy, sweet scent. Carroway cups the flower gently in his palm.

Milkweed.

SIX

The heat has become what he imagines equa-
torial heat to be. The heat of Conrad's Africa.
Kipling's India. The path to the mess hall has
baked to a ceramic hardness; the green of the
crab grass is diffuse with a powdered dust. Only
the smallest flies seem to be out, specks of black
suspended, somehow netted in the air. Bird calls
are short, tentative, exploratory; the noise touching against the heat, withdrawing. Even the
canoes, far out on the lake now, have given up
any attachment to sound, silently adrift under
the hot blue sky, the white centre of the sun.

"Burgess and MacDonald are in their element," says Adeline, her elbows on the picnic table, her hands at rest beneath her chin, her knitting bag beside her. "They're at their best when they have some responsibility. You should have heard them laying down the law to the little ones they were taking with them in their canoes."

A black beetle negotiates his way slowly along a planed log, slipping into the crevice between it and the next log, lumbering back up, pausing at the pitcher of iced tea sweating into a pool at the table's centre. Shirley Stickles lays her charcoal across his path. Journeys are never easy.

"Are those your Science Day projects?" Moisture shines the clusters of acne along her forehead, her cheeks.

"They worked on them yesterday. I always bring some books. Field guides."

"Who would have thought that Cardinal could draw?" She holds up the top Bristol board. A pressed clump of Indian paintbrush scotch-taped in a corner touches its pinks and reds, its crushed green against a line drawing of several blossoms, painstakingly-drawn brooms of petals, spear-like leaves. Adjacent is an inked sketch of an Indian head and feathered headdress, each feather carefully patterned and shaded. There is hardly room for his report which lies in a cramped block in one corner, lettered laboriously, the size of the letters diminishing as they near the cardboard edge.

"Now his spelling is something else." The young woman exposes her crooked teeth in an abrupt 'haw' of laughter. A mouth like Dean Richards' wife's at the conservatory, the two prominent front teeth at angles against each other.

"Let's see." Adeline shifts, her breasts spilling over the picnic table, her hand reaching for the chart. Scaly skin, blunt fingers. Mrs. Richards had long, shaped nails with pink lacquer on them. Was it the first time he had ever seen such nails? Claws, Malcolm called them.

"Oh, this is precious. Listen: 'In books this flower is called Common Red Paintbrush but it really should be called Indian Paintbrush unless you want to call it by its Science name' (he's spelled Science S-I-E-N-S) 'Castilleja miniata. It should be called Indian because we were here first' (F-R-I-S-T) 'You want a surprise? The red part is really leaves. The flowers is green. I couldn't find no lejun'—legend!—'but I bet there is one somewhere only maybe with the Indians and not wroten down yet.' Jack, you must have a hard time looking at these with a straight face."

"Actually I haven't really had a chance to look at them yet. They worked on them while I was resting yesterday. Thought I'd look them over while everyone's out on the lake."

"That Indian head is really very well done. Hold it up, Shirley, from where you're sitting." Adeline squints, pushing flesh close to the pale greenness of her eyes. "He must have spent a lot of time on it. You should see what West Cabin has come up with."

"I know. I know." A little shriek from Shirley of the crooked teeth. How'd you like to lock choppers with her? Malcolm's moonlit eyes, always just a shade off madness in the pre-dawn. If she asks me to sing *The Rosary* one more time I'll spill my cookies all over her party pumps. *The hours I spent with thee, dear tart.* . . . Christ. Daddy's favourite song. No reason generations should have to suffer forever. The cigarette in the dark, a small *o* of glowing ash.

"Then they put papier mâché all over a balloon and let it harden, but the tail— get this— they wanted to use Millie's small skillet. They thought it would make a perfect beaver's tail. Millie was incensed."

I count them over every one apart. The voice, diminished in the night but as perfect as the fading galaxies, the ivory moon. Then you know what happens, you've got the frigging song stuck in your mind, and you wish it was something by Schubert or even Cole Porter but it's *My Rosary, My Rosary.*

" . . . had me mixing papier mâché until I thought my arm was going to fall off. If you're wondering where all the journals went to, now you know."

Malcolm's last letter was folded around a photograph. One of those street photographs, surprise in the eyes, anonymous people on a Vancouver sidewalk. Hatted, raincoated, but nothing can hide the skeletal thinness of the hands, the neck. Eyes, the flicker of surprise, receding, cheekbones protruding. On the back is scribbled, "I'm often mistaken for Gregory Peck."

" . . . but Carroway made me promise to keep it a secret so my lips are sealed." Shirley Stickles puts her hand over her mouth. It is a sensible, well-shaped hand with the odd stainings of craftsman's dyes that do not come off with scrubbing.

Carroway?

"Surprises are so important at that age." The two women continue a lazy inventory of the Science Day charts. Burgess has copied a Korean legend of the tiger lily out of *The Legends and Lore of Wildflowers*. Something about a hermit who has removed an arrow from a tiger's paw and drowns but the tiger, in the guise of orange flowers, continues to search over the centuries for him. The lines have the ring of Fritch and Pennington. Probably nothing in the text has been changed. Shirley Stickles reads it aloud, savouring the language of legend. The drowned hermit. The final baptism. Slow descent into the still depths, air running to the surface in trails of bubbles. The urgency of the elements to cohere to their own. The body is ninety-three percent water— ninety-five? Water to water.

"Ah, here's Carroway's." The chart hides

Shirley Stickles' face. "Another artist." Then the laugh. "But possibly not."

"What do you mean?"

"Look at this." She moves closer to him, the Bristol board flat to the table. A pressed sprig of milkweed in one corner, the flower clusters enlarged in a drawing that spreads across the page, each cupped petal meticulously recreated along with the plump, hairy seed pods of the mature plant. A butterfly settles on one flower cluster, the design of his wings elaborate and carefully detailed. "Does that style look familiar?"

"Cardinal?"

"I'd be willing to bet." The eyes behind the horn-rimmed glasses flicker back and forth over Carroway's report. "But the writing is definitely Carroway's: 'The Common Milkweed. *Asclepias syriaca.* Asklepios was the Greek god of medicine, and, at one time, it was thought that the milkweed had powerful medicinal value. In fact, the milkweed is more of a murderer than a healer.'" The words hum in the afternoon, like a litany, a chant of definition. "'A close look at the blossoms will show that what appears to be the petals are in reality hood-like outgrowths of the tube formed by the joined filaments of the five stamens. The actual petals form another tube with reddish lobes. At the base of this column are nectar glands hidden by pink, erect hoods growing from the base. If you push one of the hoods back, you will see a slender, curved horn'."

"He's been into Fritch and Pennington too."

Stickles is determined in her reading. She noses closer to the text. "That may be, but hold on. Let's see: 'Inside of each little milkweed flower, between the nectar flasks, are five slits with the plant's pollen massed within them. An insect, crawling over the flower in search of nectar, often, to gain a foothold, places its feet in the tiny slit-like openings. When it has drunk its fill of nectar and prepares to fly away, it may find that, as it struggles to become airborne, its feet slide upwards in the slits which are narrower at the top than at the bottom. Some will struggle free; others will find themselves held so tightly they give up the struggle and die.'" Traps of satiation. All laid out by God, Malcolm would say. The Big Joker waiting with a noose. That's if you believe in God. Do you, Jack? Not waiting for an answer. Sometimes I don't. The voice for a moment soft, even wistful. Shirley Stickles is laughing. "Surely this isn't out of your flower encyclopedia. Carroway has to have made this up. Listen: 'A Transylvanian legend tells us that the milkweed came into being when some handsome princes were transformed by an evil vampire fairy. The evil vampire fairy, who was jealous of their youth and beauty, said, "Forever after you will be a weed of the field and the milk white of your skin will bleed from broken stems." But a good fairy turned the bad one into an ugly insect who crawled upon the flower because of its sweet smell, sucking the nectar glands, sucking here and sucking there the pink, erect hoods until he was so big and heavy that he couldn't take off. When he tried to flap his ugly wings and leave, he found out his feet were caught in the flower's slits. He struggled and struggled. . . . '"

A flicker of pain like the darting tongue of a snake along the base of his skull. His head going forward toward the papers, the dampened stains, the beetle crawling back along the same precarious path. He can stop his head's descent. He can force his eyes up to the blazing sky. Moisture leaving his body along the entire surface of his skin in a wave of release, soothing, cooling. Small rivers run along his forehead, well against the bridge of his nose, the frames of his glasses. His hands hold the edge of the table.

Adeline Tupper's trill of soprano laughter seems to come from a great distance. "What an imagination! Are you okay, Jack?" The voice comes closer. "Have some more iced tea. Well, it was iced. Lukewarm now, I guess."

The canoes have returned to shore. There is a hubbub of voices softened in the heat.

"It was nice while it lasted," Adeline sighs. They rise, almost as if strings have attached them to the hovering sounds. Tupper and Bragge and McEvoy are coming up the hill, the boys drifting to their cabins, or sticking to the lakeshore, the sand, the dock, the beached canoes.

The picnic table shudders as the swimming instructor heaves himself onto the bench.

"What a day." He pats his chest pocket for cigarettes.

"Like glass." Tupper eases himself onto the other end of the bench. "I've never seen the lake so still. I swear you could see to the bottom."

The twin boys circle languidly in each other's arms, staring at one another wide-eyed with the clarity of death. Are they smiling? The whisper of some secret knowledge pulling at their lips, betraying the pearl teeth. Hair swaying like fine seaweed. Fish nibble, daintily carnivorous. Engorged leeches rest on the pale skin. The hands hold, the legs entwine, the mirrored eyes draw in the horizonless expanse, the pellucid dusk of the lakebottom, the terrible twilight.

"Not leaving, Jack? Have a cigarette." Braggc imperils the picnic bench, leans over with his opened packet, one smoke shaken up.

"I shouldn't." But he takes it. Bragge's meaty fingers strike a match. A whiff of sulphur moves against the heavy sweetness of citronella and sweat. He sits back down, holding the smoke in his chest until it seems to become a part of himself. Terry McEvoy manoeuvres his bronze legs over the seat next to him. In the heat, he wears nothing but his swim briefs. His torso is slick with sweat and oil and insect repellant.

"And how were Burgess and MacDonald?" Adeline has come back with a new pitcher of iced tea.

"Fantastic." McEvoy accepts his tea with a

boyish eagerness that seems to make her expand and glow. "They were just great."

"We ended up putting Cardinal in charge of one of the canoes too. You would've thought he was chief of the reservation." Tupper bolts his glass of tea and then begins cracking the ice in his teeth. "It just goes to show."

Shirley Stickles settles back down on the other side of McEvoy, her face reddening. She holds the glass for a moment against her cheek. McEvoy begins to set his down on Carroway's chart.

"Oops. We better move these." She seems grateful to have something to do and stacks them against the end of the table. "Don't want to damage North Cabin's masterpieces. Carroway's is something else."

"I don't know how you do it, Jack." The minister mops his forehead with a stained handkerchief. "I tried to get my crew moving on rocks, you know. So far they've identified Mexican turquoise, two black diamonds, a piece of rare jade and a chunk of amethyst. The amethyst is a piece of telephone-line conductor glass, and the rest you can imagine."

Amethyst, he remembers, was his mother's birthstone. The brooch she wore into the ground, a glinting purple-eyed peacock, its metal feathers fanning against the cream lace of wedding finery, handcrafted lace, slack with age, brown-spotted like her folded hands. The dress cut up the back to fit over the fatness of the woman in the coffin. Coffin nails, she called cigarettes. I blame that young man, that Malcolm, for getting you started. Moisture rimming her eyes, her lips quivering, drawing back from her teeth. It killed your father I'm sure. That vile pipe, always hanging from his mouth. Only she could see a connection between tobacco and a ruptured appendix. She cried often and openly, setting her sorrow against the world, her teacup on the kitchen table, wild roses in a yellow vase, pale crockery and checkered curtains. Things in their place.

"I guess we're pretty well set for Sports Day tomorrow." Tupper speaks around an ice cube in his mouth. "I think we'll get started right after breakfast." Two of the younger boys have moved up from the lake and are playing a lazy game of tag in a wide circle around the picnic table.

"They should probably all go for a swim before supper." McEvoy arches his face to the sky, hunches his shoulders forward and then wings them back so that the muscles ripple. From inside there is a sound of satisfied cracking as sinew and bone move and settle. "Whaddya say, Shirl, in for a dip?" He starts to get up, stares for an instant with dismay at the straining bulge in his briefs, resettles himself quickly on the bench. "Think I'll have another swig of that tea."

The ebb and flow of blood. Floodgates somewhere in the mind. A nerve somewhere, like a filament of down on the stem of a crocus.

Endlessly twitching. Hanged men die with hard-ons. Damndest thing you've ever seen in your life. Grahame Washburne releasing a stream against brownstained porcelain in the Legion Hall men's room. They hung these three collaborators. Some little town in Africa. Hell, I can't remember. Hung them from one of them balcony railings. Damned if someone hadn't pulled the pants off one of them and there he is dangling and his cock sticking straight out. You could've hung your hat on it.

"I told Millie to go for a cold supper tonight." Frank Tupper chases a last ice cube around the bottom of the pitcher. "Potato salad."

The cigarette has burned close to his fingers. One last pull of smoke from the packed, burning leaves. His breath shudders as he draws it in. The wash of perspiration has settled into his clothing.

"I'll take those, Miss Stickles." He holds the charts away from the dampness of his body. His knees have no strength but it is possible to keep balance by moving slowly, putting one foot consciously in front of the other, moving along the packed clay path.

The boys are in the cabin. Potherby asleep, curled fetally on his bunk blanket. MacDonald, in undershorts, is face down on his cot, his arms dangling over the edges, fingers grazing the floor. Burgess lies on his back, looking at a *Mad* magazine. Cardinal and Bowmeister and Wesley are at the table drawing. Carroway, moving around the room, smiles his half smile.

"Hey, Mr. Hislop." Cardinal holds up his drawing. "See this here eagle." The same meticulous detailing as on the Indian headdress.

"Chief's learning us how to draw birds." Bowmeister has copied the eagle's head, getting it all wrong, the eyes askew of the beak.

"We're impressed with your craftsmanship, Cardinal." He leans the Bristol boards against the wall. "Miss Stickles and Mrs. Tupper think you have the makings of an artist. I second their opinion. You really should sign the work you did on Carroway's chart though."

Cardinal, flushing, begins working through the pattern on another eagle feather.

Carroway's eyes widen, the dilated pupils pushing black against the grey circles. If he laughs, it is softly, deep inside his throat.

"Mr. McEvoy thinks you should all go for a quick swim before supper." There is a stir of movement, papers abandoned, clothes discarded on the floor. "Perhaps you could stay back for a minute, Carroway."

Potherby is the last to leave, shaken out of his sleep, almost crying. The screen door slams.

Carroway has changed into grey trunks that seem to have been woven of irridiscent threads. He sits on the edge of his bunk, hugging his knees, the smile less than the half smile, the eyes unwavering, like unconscious waters, a force in themselves, without mediation.

"You want to search through my stuff again?"

On the table: the eye of the eagle, the beak, the talon.

"It's all a game to you, isn't it?" His voice quavers, one more betrayal of the body.

"A game?"

"I think you know what I mean."

The lips don't move. There is no sound.

"I'm not sure what you're up to, Carroway, but I want you to know that I'm watching you. You only need one more demerit."

The chin tilts. The golden shoulders shrug.

The stab again at the base of his skull. Tea moves from his stomach back to his throat, acid and burning. His hand gestures in the direction of the lake, dismissive. The door closing behind Carroway signals a new release of pain, across the chest, along the shoulders, something caught and wrenching. The pill bottle is empty on the nightstand. He is standing outside of himself, watching himself move, an old man lurching to the door, gasping for air in the torrid, airless afternoon, groping from tree to tree until his feet touch the gravel of the parking lot. His hand is on the car door, opening, releasing the captured heat, turning the catch on the glove compartment. Fits of trembling. The small bottle dancing before he can force it to stillness, remove the cap, place the pill inside his mouth. Who is this old man? When did he become old? The ribbed plush rises up to meet his hand-skin, his face-skin. Eyes close. A service for the dead, the closing of eyes. The pain eases its grip, still present— but coy. The eyes will open again but it is good to lean back, leave them closed. When it is possible, he looks through the windshield and its veil of dust. The trees move back into place, the bulk of the hall, the roofs of the cabins. His leg extends; his foot tests the gravel. He is crying; he can hear himself crying, feel the shudders in his chest. There is no emotion, just a release, an easing. He is not crying for the smoothskinned boy in the casket, the old women of his life. He is not crying for the young man coughing blood or the wide-eyed teenagers dancing in their slow underwater embrace. Slowly it stops. He is not crying. His body seems to have given up its last ounce of moisture. Mrs. Washburne would be horrified at the state of his clothes. In chiffoniere drawers, pyjamas lie folded, as carefully pressed as flowers in the pages of the dictionary. His robe, smelling of soap and air, is draped over one arm of the wooden butler. Cotton sheets, like snow, are turned back against a patterned quilt. *Make my bed and light the light, I'll arrive late tonight.* Both feet on the gravel, the world has stopped spinning. Equilibrium in little buttons of compressed powder. No wonder doctors exude such a sense of power. Grodey's pen against paper; the ink transfusion. But how many miracles per customer?

He finds it possible to make his way back to the cabin without the support of trees.

SEVEN

That evening there is no bonfire. The thought of adding to the heat is more than anyone can bear. Once again, John Hislop foregoes his supper and sleeps while the others eat. He nods off again, later, in the staffroom easy chair while Tupper and Bragge play cribbage. The minister finally shakes him awake so that he can return to the cabin and go to bed properly. The boys, despite the humidity, are all asleep except for Carroway who lies too still, posing, the slightest smile on his lips. The rest have given in to heat and exhaustion. Potherby and Bowmeister are lost in the darkest part of the cabin. MacDonald, again in undershorts, covers kicked away, snores, a steady resonant snoring that is echoed in snorts and snuffles by Wesley curled against his own pillow. Burgess is quiet, lying on his stomach, his face turned, unconscious, like a swimmer seeking air.

The Indian boy is on the bunk nearest the table. He lies, uncovered, face up, his mouth open and from time to time there is a sound, like an aah that catches, held in the throat and then sometimes released and sometimes just lost. His undershorts are what Mrs. Washburne calls tattletale grey. Every once in a while an outflung hand twitches like the spasm in the limb of a sleeping dog.

Vernon Hubbard's *A Fieldguide to Prairie Wildflowers* is open on the table at a picture of jewelweed, the small fire-flowers dusted with purple. *Impatiens capensis.* Found where there is moisture or shade, jewelweed or touch-me-not, as it is more commonly known, may be distinguished by its pendant orangey-gold blossoms spotted with purple.

Cardinal. Dejarlais. Hair sleek-black, damp against the greyish pillow. Fitful, even feverish. The eyes open suddenly, seeing beyond all consciousness.

I don't feel so good.

But what did the eyes see? What horror did they see? The night window gives him back himself. For a long time, he looks at his reflection in the glass as if, hidden in the configuration of greying hair and dark-rimmed glasses, the mouth pressed closed, the long fingers of his left hand clasped over his chin, there is an answer, something not immediately apparent like those hidden pictures in children's books where, if you stare long enough, a snake uncoils from the leaves of a tree, a fairy emerges from the water reeds, a hawk darts from the coils of a cloud. He has a mouth that is a stranger to laughter; laughter has always been painful and choking. Christ, you're a barrel, Malcolm had thrown up his hands after they had roomed together for a week. A barrel? Yeah, a barrel of laughs. Luck of the draw that I get Lon Chaney for a room-mate. What! What's this? A smile, the face is crackin', I don't believe it. Opening the window and shouting out to the compound below: the Phantom of the Opera has smiled and all's swell.

The seed pod, Hubbard continues, is comprised of five valves. Deceptive in its maturity, because it is still green, the pod will explode at the slightest touch, scattering a multitude of seeds. Hence its common name.

There had been no ice in the camp but one of the boys fetched a pail of cold spring water. He pressed a cloth wrung out in it against the boy's hot forehead and, in time, Dejarlais fell asleep, a restless, anxious sleep. It's the best thing, my love, if you can just sleep, his mother's voice strange and distant as if through water. But her hand is close and large and the washcloth cool against his cheek. In the morning you'll be all better. Do you want me to sing to you? Softly, so softly. *Lullaby and goodnight, with roses bedight, with lilies bespread is Jackie's wee bed.*

Sleeping. Waking. Why is his hand on the boy's shoulder? Skin, sinew, bone. His fingers tracing. The boy's eyes are closed but he turns and tosses. Parts of sentences spring from his lips like the beads of sweat along his forehead. *Why can't I go? . . . the show's gonna start . . . the show. . . .* Other fragments but those over and over again.

Odd that he can still remember.

You seen him last. The mother came to him on the street a few weeks after the funeral, puffed with drunkenness, slack with grief. She wore her outward signs of decay almost with pride: a blouse buttoned to the wrong buttonholes; her hair pushed by leaning or sleep into an odd flatness on one side; her skirt hem uneven, trailing threads.

The revrun said you seen him last. Did he talk to you?

Talk?

He was my baby. Tears streaming along her flat cheeks. She opened her mouth, gasping for air, or maybe to let a soundless cry escape. *I let him go to your Jesuschrist camp and they bring him home in a box.* Her hand fastened onto his jacket collar. He could smell the beery exhalation of her breath, see the teeth flecked with decay.

Didn't he say nothing?

He said, and he told her this because other words wouldn't come, he said, "I can't go to the show."

God, he loved going to the picture show. Sometimes his dad wouldn't let him. Sonuvabitchin drunk. The hand would not release his collar. He could feel her strength as it tightened its hold. Goddam mean sonuvabitch. Didn't want no coffin with white silky stuff inside. I said that's the one we're getting and I don't give a fuck if it takes us a year to pay for it.

It was a beautiful coffin.

The words come back. He can feel his hand going to hers against his jacket, feel its odd delicacy, its fine smoothness. She released it into his. The hand of the woman. He felt something then and now, a sympathy of blood, a terrible knowledge.

He was a beautiful boy—a fine young man. He made her an offering of trite words and she looked bewildered for a moment, as if wondering how to gather them to herself. A high, keening sound came from her throat, a sound issuing from beyond time, eerie with racial memory. It made him gasp. He can feel the gasp now, still in his throat.

Cardinal moans and stirs on his bunk, drawing his knees up. The troubled sleep. An inheritance? Aboriginal? How then was Malcolm's so like it?

Lemme buy you a drink?

He had started away. His instinct was to hurry, as if he hadn't heard her, but he turned against it, turned back to her, yielding to an omnipresent guilt, heavy as that summer afternoon, heavy as this evening. Jewelweed burns on the table. His hand trembles. His face flashes in the dark window. For an instant the cabin is silent, every breath held, the world without sound, a caught film that will burn in a moment from the heat of the bulb, celluloid melting into brown-edged bubbles. And then darkness.

There is whimpering, a soft, feral noise from one of the far cots. Potherby? It intensifies, language trying to break through, failing, fading. The night continues. The page turns. St. John's wort: butter-flowers in clusters. Closed buds tinged with red. The inescapable reds: fruit, flower, fire. Mrs. Dejarlais wore red earrings, circles of glowing plastic that scattered in reflection along the beer glasses.

You drove him. She looked as if she were searching for connections, reasons, something that made sense. You come and got him in that black car.

He nodded.

I felt a shiver on my body when I seen that shiny black. . . .

I must go, he said.

Tell me.

But he left after a minute, escaping with what he could not tell. There is a shout from a nearby cabin, followed by laughter and an adult voice, low, admonishing. The night is black against the screen door. His hand pushes against the wire mesh, eases the door closed behind him. The sky is black and starless, holding the heat close to the earth. His eyes grow night-wary enough to pick out shapes: a jackpine against the quiet lake, the next cabin where there is a flash of light through the window and then darkness again. From the woods there is a sound of quick, furtive scurrying in the bushes and then the steady communal croaking of frogs, faint with lethargy and heat.

Moisture emanates from his armpits, his groin, along his shoulders again. It would be wise to get out of his clothing and into bed, hang the shirt and trousers to dry as they will. St. John's wort flickers and dies with the lantern click. Is Carroway still awake? His hands pull the curtain out full alongside his bunk, find the metal hangers on the wall-nail. For a moment he is naked, the heavy warm air against all parts of him except where the soles of his feet make contact with the linoleum rug by his bed. His fingers move along the damp concave hollow of his stomach, affirm the moist pendencies of sex below. He towels, finds crisp, folded pyjama bottoms, eases himself on top of the covers.

Sometimes the face of Mrs. Dejarlais becomes

the face of the other Indian woman although, of course, they were not really much alike. When he closes his eyes their cheeks fuse, the almond eyes overlap, the hair coils or unfolds. Mrs. Dejarlais and his one woman of the night.

Money sticks crisply out of the torn envelope in Malcolm's hand, a fan of greens and blues.

A little graduation gift from the mater, he chuckles, waving the envelope back and forth, and we, my friend, are going to number one (elevating an index finger) get us a little hooch and two (another finger) get us a little cooch.

What did they look like at eighteen? Only a couple of years older than MacDonald or Burgess. Both of them too skinny. Malcolm full of bluster and bravado in his green suit, his hair longer and curlier than anyone was wearing it then, twenty dollars in his pocket. Himself in his father's made-over jacket and grey flannels itching against his legs, his collar too tight. Long-faced and serious, his hair laid back with brilliantine. Glasses: he would be blind without them. His heart pounding high in his chest.

The beer parlour is full of noise and smoke greased with the moisture flying from the tap brew and the smell of urine from a washroom close to their table. He can see his face in a mirror, trying to look nonchalant. Malcolm lighting a cigarette. They are both underage.

He had thought up reasons not to come, all of which had left Malcolm helpless with laughter.

You've never had yourself a piece!

Have you?

You're talking to someone who busted the old cherry at age fifteen and three months.

Sure.

Doubt— if you will.

It is never possible to tell with Malcolm. He lies effortlessly, with a smooth companionable ease. Whatever blend of fabrication and conspiratorial friendliness he uses with the beer-parlour waiter seems to work. The waiter listens, shrugs his shoulders and accepts money.

After the closing call, they wait in the alley until he comes out. Both of them are filled with three hours of beer, their eyes streaming from smoke. The waiter looks small and mean in his coat and hat. They nod and he gestures for them to follow. A warm night of early summer. Malcolm half-humming, half-singing of all things *The Rosary*, maybe not so self-assured as he is trying to appear. They make their way unsteadily, hands sometimes reaching out for the security of a telephone pole, a brick wall, the board encasement of a fire escape.

Hold it, mate. Only Malcolm would use a word like "mate," gleaned from novels and some odd sense of Britishness. The waiter lights a cigarette as the young man fumbles with his fly, and, sighing, releases a stream of beery piss against a decaying wall. The need is in himself too, but in front of the unwavering yellow-eyed glare of the waiter he cannot.

Odd how much of life is spent reliving what has already gone before. To walk down those alleys a thousand times—what purpose? what design? Are there people who live outside of memory in a kind of relief through initiative? Forward peddling instead of always back. When he was eighteen and moving woozily through the night channels of experience, was his mind hooked even then, seeing his mother's hand brush the petal onto an incomplete, still-wet rose; watching Mrs. Carey tilt her birdlike face toward a biscuit tin filled with silhouettes clipped from magazines; holding in his mind the young man singing, soft-lit in the hall of hushed faces and shining wood and leaded glass? Or does he, being eighteen, only think I've got to pee but I won't in front of the yellow-eyed waiter?

On the floor of his study, he had felt them, the heavy clustering of relived thoughts and images, and then he felt them seeping away so that there was only the now of the piano leg with its brass claw, and the little animal screeches of the youngest Wilson girl who had forgotten to practice, and the strange blue flowers on the rug. Finally Mrs. Washburne's busy feet. It was a release in pain, but his life didn't flash before him, only Mrs. Washburne's black, perforated shoes and rolled-down stockings. For days there was nothing— or was there? Maybe it has simply escaped him.

His days in the hospital were almost without

memory. He lived as the lower animals do, in the present with only the residual memory of the species, the instinct to move, to eat, to fear the unseen beyond the door. Nurses came in and put glass into his mouth and cold rubber vise-like around his arm and pressed their fingers against his wrist.

Elsie Panek talked about the crowd down at the Legion, how they were fed up with radio music and Mort McGilvery murdering the piano accordian. Another nurse made it her mission to keep him posted on the weather. That was his world: the cheerful words, the practical moves, the still, floral curtains, the pale walls like unripe apples. From his bed, the sky was a rectangle cut through with a window sash. Sometimes the blueness was smudged with clouds; sometimes it was cast in grey. Food came under domed steel lids. Sometimes he ate a bite.

As his strength came back, the memories began to return, visiting dreams, rustling through his waking hours. Sometimes it seemed his mother came and sat with him, as she had when he had first come down with rheumatic fever. She wore her amethyst brooch, knowing that he liked it. If he reached out to touch her, though, her arm became the sweatered arm of Mrs. Washburne who sat slyly in her place, reading or sewing.

There are things to remember but he has found only some of them; the others wait in the black car, in the campfire voices. Where else? If there are ghosts, maybe this is what they are: what the mind sees in the July grass, the muskeg, the spark-wheeling night. They wait.

An owl hoots and there is silence and then it hoots again. MacDonald's interrupted snoring continues. One of the boys coughs. There is a touch of cooler air moving from the window screen beneath the glass to the screen door. He can only guess at the time: it must be midnight or after.

His eyes close. The Indian woman whispers, Tell me. But where is the language to tell her how the boy's shoulders looked with sunshine on them through the car window? His fingers have always been more eloquent. He can see himself inviting her over to the Legion so he can play *Liebestraum* for her. *My dream of love was meant to live forever.* But Roy Dejarlais was not meant to live even the proper span of years. On the night before he died, his fingers memorized the boy's features as if they, if nothing else, anticipated his death.

She closes her mouth. The face becomes placid, a moon, the hair coiled, the eyes half asleep. There are two of them.

Christ, Malcolm whispers, he didn't tell me they were squaws.

This here's Stella. The waiter gestures to the smaller one closer to the stairway.

My size, Malcolm laughs, giving a hitch to his green pants. He heads toward her.

Bernice. The waiter's thumb points back at the other. She is in a housecoat with trails of fringe but some of the fringe is missing. When Malcolm and Stella have disappeared, she starts up the staircase. He follows. Her slippers are scuffed and one of the heels looks like it might fall off. They go down a short hall to a bedroom.

So? she says, clicking on a lamp with a yellow paper shade. It lights the room only dimly. She is a woman beginning to be heavy, maybe ten years older than himself although it is hard to tell.

Name's Jack. His laugh sounds silly and small-boyish. She arches an eyebrow. It has been plucked almost free of hair and reconstructed in a thin, dark line. Jack Hislop.

Hislop. She explores the word accenting the second syllable. Hiss slop. He hates the name. It sounds fussy and common.

She chuckles deep in her throat. He can feel the blood rushing to his face. Maybe you better get out of some of those Sunday school clothes. You be more comfortable. She unties the kimona and slips it off. Her breasts are unlike any that he's seen in the fine-arts prints in the college library. These are not small and strawberry-tipped. They are pendulous with large brownish-red aureoles and dark, puckered nipples. The hair between her legs is as sleek and dark as an otter's. The springs of the bed creak as she lies down.

You're going to have to take off more than your necktie and one shoe.

He strips quickly and is surprised that his cock has leapt out, engorged.

Now that's what I like to see, she laughs again, softly, in the back of her throat, and extends her hand to him. He lies beside her, her flesh against him, her breasts against his chest, his cock straight against his belly, her belly, and there is the smell of sweat and a kind of perfume that he has never smelled before.

It's better if you lie on top of me. Her hand takes hold of him, guiding him between her legs until he is in. He lies there hard and full of himself, in the warm, wet enfoldment of her flesh and he can see her eyes, naked with hurt for an instant until she realizes he is looking at her.

You gotta do more, lover, she whispers in his ear. You gotta move.

He thrusts and the bedsprings creak wildly.

Oh God, she says, don't stop.

He keeps thrusting, his elbows burning, the hardness stretched out, the tension coiled in him, unable to release. Her hands knead his back, flutter along his buttocks, claw his shoulders. He lies quiet in her for a moment, streaming sweat.

Suddenly she screams, a small hissing scream. Danny, get back to bed.

He twists his torso and over his shoulder he can see the boy in the doorway. He is half asleep, naked except for some tattered underwear.

His cock shrivels back to himself and she slides out from under him and grabs the kimono. The boy is beautiful and golden. He rubs at sleep in his eyes. She hurries him out into the hall and he is left alone in the room, wet with perspiration, his bladder ready to burst.

It is Malcolm who appears in the doorway.

Here lies one busted cherry if I ever saw one, he chortles.

He is dressed by the time Bernice comes back. Malcolm pats her on the shoulder. You done a good deed tonight, sweetheart. She doesn't look at Malcolm, though. She looks at him, almost sadly.

Come back again, Jack.

Christ, you told her your name. They are in the alley outside and he can finally piss. It seems to take five minutes.

Why not?

I don't know. I told Stella my name was Rudolph. Of course I was thinking of Valentino. There is the sound of his laughter and a couple of cars moving on the street at the end of the alley. Malcolm's arm is across his shoulder in a buddy grasp, as if they are playing a scene in a show where drunken friends stagger home together. Singing. *No one here can love or understand me. . . .*

EIGHT

John Hislop, lying on his cot, can feel the accu-
mulation of nights from past years like the folds
of the silver-threaded curtains. He can almost
touch them and for that reason, perhaps, he
keeps his hands flat against his blanket. It is a
long time before he sleeps, with the nocturnal
murmurings of the dormitory in his ears,
whispering, reminding, but when he does give in
to sleep, it is not the conservatory that spills into
his unconsciousness, but the chapel of the Jack-
son Funeral Parlour. Charlton Morris, the funeral
director, cups one hand under his elbow while

the other sweeps in the direction of three coffins. I got a deal, you see, Morris whispers. Brown polished wood, open lids revealing puckered white satin buttoned into place. Bulk orders. . . .

The piano is on a dais to the side. It is ebony black. Morris steers him with his pudgy undertaking hand. Whatever you think would be appropriate, he continues whispering. We don't like to be too formal at the viewings, you know. Put people at their ease, that's the way nowadays. An upright, it blocks his view of the coffins. His fingers fall into the introduction to *None But the Lonely Heart*, the chords satisfying and dull like winter sunshine or porridge. Mrs. Washburne in her coat trimmed with a scruffy, glass-eyed fox leans against the piano humming. The melody changes almost imperceptibly into *In the Garden. And He walks with me and He talks with me*, she trills. Adeline Tupper comes up, heavy in red tartan. Her fingers graze his shoulder and although the touch is light and tentative, he can sense a sympathy in it. Frank wonders if you'd play something the boys know since they all came. He softens the closing notes of *In the Garden* to a whisper of their own and then leads in, just as softly, to the melody of *Boom, Boom, Ain't it Great to be Crazy?* He plays it in slow march tempo, something he's always been good at, turning a waltz into a fox trot or a tango. Playing *Three Blind Mice* in a boogie woogie beat. *Twinkle, Twinkle, Little Star* eight to the bar. Thanks, Jack. She squeezes his shoulder again and retreats

awkwardly in red sandals. He plays faster and
faster, a sound building inside himself with a terrible pressure so that finally he is gasping, tears
running down his face, spittle flying from his
mouth. Mrs. Washburne hoists her slipping fox.
Sat on a tombstone shooting dice. He can't keep
the laughter out—listen, Malcolm!—and it races
out of his mouth. He whirls away from the piano.
The boys are filing past the caskets. They are
holding flowers: tiger lilies, fireweed, buttercups.
They all look scrubbed and uncomfortable in
their Sunday clothing and slicked-back hair. Carroway, smiling, with milkweed in his hands.

The shuddering laughter has stopped. Everyone looks at him expectantly. He moves to the
first coffin. Malcolm lies in quietness, his great
eyes lidded, his auburn hair formed into perfect
curls lapping against his wax ears, his alabaster
skin. Charlton Morris sighs: really so young and
such fine hands (crossed on his green suit jacket)
and, the voice lowering to an almost inaudible
confidentiality, do you know he was erect if you
get my drift. That's the first time I've ever seen
that (a terrible, suppressed whinnying of
laughter), a stiff on a stiff.

Someone is fooling around playing chopsticks
on the piano, the coupled notes tentative and
untimed. Not too loud now, boys, says Charlton
Morris. Mrs. Dejarlais is smoothing the satin lin-
ing of the second coffin. Frank Tupper has sidled
up to her. A terrible thing, he says, unable to
make his voice soft. But Jesus has him on his

team now. Mrs. Dejarlais' mouth opens in a howl. Fucking Christ, what have they done to him? I lightened him up a bit, says Charlton Morris, but you may want to touch up his hair.

Mrs. Steinhauer brings in a tub of sandwiches. Her special devilled egg. The boys quit playing chopsticks and flock around her. Okay, hollers Tupper, there's lots for everyone. No need to push. Who threw that? The shriek of his whistle. We don't want any devilled egg in the caskets and I don't want to see any more food wasted. I think all you boys better go outside. How about you, Jack? Going to have one of Millie's masterpieces? Proteinous yellow crumbs along his lips, stuck to his teeth.

He refuses, and waits for the right moment to slip out. But it is dark now. How has it become so late? His hands feel the branches of trees, his feet move steadily along the sand path toward the cabin. No light is on. Maybe the boys will be asleep, or else telling whispered jokes or just laughing for no reason the way teenagers do. The cabin is so quiet, there is not even the sound of breathing. All under the blankets are dead to the world. Now if the Indian boy has no fever . . . but his bed is empty, the covers in disarray, trailing onto the floor still damp from the boy's streaming sweat. Oh God, where is he? There's no one in the toilets. Back to the cabin. But the bed is empty.

The bed is empty.

He is awake with a jolt, his eyes drinking in the darkness. There is an alien sound and then he realizes: rain on the roof. A welcome coolness from the still-open window, the still-open door. Thunder rumbles distantly. But there is something more than the quiet thunder and the quiet rain, some knowledge of the night that he can't apprehend, something secret and withheld. He must fight for it, fight off the dream, the warm cocoon of sleep. Something in the cabin itself. It is too dark to see. Something in the air.

It is the silence, a heavy deadness enveloped by the walls, no sound of breathing beyond the thudding in his own chest. If he listens long enough there will be the creak of a cot spring, a word lost from a dream into the night air, a resumed snore. But he waits and there is nothing— only the softly drumming rain, the rolling away of thunder beyond the lake.

With a heave like a swimmer fighting upward to break the surface of the water, his body wrests itself from sleep, from the bed. The floor smooth and cool on his feet; he can feel where water has come in through the window. The camp lamp, switched to light, blinds him and then, out of its yellow glow, yields the flaring St. John's wort, a moth husk, his glasses, the stack of Science Day charts.

The bed of the Indian boy is empty.

His heart stops.

The bed is empty.

Is he meant to live out the scene again? Run a flashlighted course through the woods, picking up the startled birds in his beam, a flash of fireweed, the rasping green of jackpines. The muskeg and the oozing moss easing the boy's burning nakedness. Breathing against clumps of marsh grass, his face in profile, one eye wide on the searchers, the eye of an animal or a bird that has given in to the knowledge of its death.

The bed is empty.

All of the beds are empty. Every one of them, bedding and sleeping bags in disarray. A pair of undershorts by a cot leg, pyjama bottoms crumpled in a mass by the door. Like a trail.

Outside the rain is falling with gentleness, barely a drizzle. The sand path is wet and cool against the soles of his feet. There are bursts of laughter from the lake, intermittent— and hushed calling back and forth. Rain has drawn them to the lake, sky and earth as water. Faces are held up to the cooling rain; bodies are lifted in the warm, mothering force of the lake water.

The drizzle eases into mist and frayed clouds allow the light of a sodden moon. It gives the boys in the lake a kind of ghostliness as they bob up and down in the water. In himself he feels the ache of memory: racing with his cousins over a wet beach, embracing the water as summer rain pelted down in darkness.

Are you crazy? his Aunt Florence hollering. You want to be struck by lightning?

He is close enough to hear what they are calling to one another. As figures, though, they have
no separateness; they are like pale creatures from
another world, moon children, a species without
differentiation.

"You're it, Chief." One of the smaller boys
calls out. Potherby? They are playing water tag,
leaping as high as they can out of the water,
plunging back down in great splashes.

"You missed me."

"No I didn't."

"Suck my cock."

Ripples of laughter. More leaping. They are
creating small waves that roll in to the sand and
touch his feet with amorphic patches of foam.
One of the older boys— Burgess? MacDonald?— is
the first to sense his presence.

"Oh shit." The others catch the changed note
in the voice and soon they are all quiet in the
water, watching him.

"Hey, Mr. Hislop," Bowmeister calls out. "You
should feel how warm the water is."

"I know." His own voice is a kind of hoarse
whisper that seems to belong to someone else.
"But it's very late."

They straggle onto the beach, shining and
naked; the soft moonlight gives them an animal
gracefulness. They flick the water from themselves like ponies, race off toward the cabin. Carroway is the last out. He is different— he does not

have the animal innocence of the others. He moves through the moonlight with the awareness of someone watching himself in a mirror, conscious of the flash of knee, the slim night-whiteness of his torso, the soft configuration of his sex. Their eyes do not meet.

He will give them time to get back into bed. What his body craves most is a cigarette. He can feel his heart still racing, a vein ticking at his temple. The empty sweat-drenched bed whirls in his mind. Why can't the mind steady the cot, smooth the covers, find the crying boy, dry his face, carry him back to life? There is no past reality except for what lies in the mind, so why can this not be done? Why must his hands move forever through the crisscross of flashlight beams, reaching toward the figure, the golden-brown living skin slaked with sweat and marsh mud—move toward but never connect because the voice cries out, a hysterical animal cry running against the sudden silence of the night, crying out over and over again.

Don't touch me.

And the look of loathing and horror on the streaked face, the body trying to burrow into the mud and water.

Don't touch me. It becomes a refrain that loses itself in choked crying.

I'd better carry him, says Reverend Smight.

The loons have come out with the rain and thunder gone. Birds of mystic power to the

Indians. Of course the boy was out of his mind with fever but in the burning he saw— what?— the desire, the unadmitted longing, sensed the pleasure in the fingers moving a cool cloth against his forehead, gently along the cheek, the arched neck, trailing to the shoulder, the arm. How many times has he relived the night? A resolve that he had in the light of day, a resolve that nature had taken its own perverse course and that he had only been a bit-player in the scene, the man who carries in the basin, the wet cloths, the towels, that resolve can change in the night, in the long hours of trying to fall asleep, in the sleepless time when dreams jerk him awake and there is still the rest of the night to be lived through. At such times, the scene can offer itself in different ways. Sometimes an insistent spotlight bathes the boy so that attention is drawn to the smallest detail, as a body is viewed on an operating table in a hospital theatre. There are no shadows. His fingers touch the black hair stranded with sweat, the full lips, the fragile construction of neck and shoulders, skin over the delicate, developing bones; touch the small peak of the larynx and, moving down, touch the nipples on his chest, those small, strange vestiges of femininity. His fingers note the sealed umbilical scar, brush over the contours of the sex caught in the damp undershorts, sex that has begun to react to imprints of change, the penis beginning to show its fullness, part of a testicle revealed from the frayed leg of the undershorts, the soft crimping of flesh over seed pod. Touch the slim brown-gold legs, the smooth, boyish upper thighs, the bone-defined shanks, the intricate webbing of bones in the feet.

Sometimes there is no stage lighting, just a soft insistence of the moon or maybe a false dawn. His hand moves with the damp cloth warming to the fever temperature, the hand resting against the forehead, a cheek, the chest with its turmoil of breathing. And yet the nerves in his fingers sending signals that set the blood coursing, that stiffen the phallus. His body becomes hollow, his head light, whirling around the probing phallus. The fingers tremble. The cloth drops and—does he, does he feel with his fingers the sweat-slaked skin, travel the forbidden routes? Perhaps if the mind can conjure the thought, that is enough. The verdict is guilty. Yes. He accepts it. He had been almost faint with desire—that is the truth—but it had been a formless, terrible desire. Only the mind since has been able to give it form, to define the unacceptable, to expand the guilt until it is full-blown, epic. Yes, guilty, every day of his life. Can there be more punishment than memory and the mind's knowledge of possibility?

The boy died.

Other boys came and slept in the bed. In the other beds. He did not trust his fingers against them. Even if he touched them by accident, he drew back quickly.

The boy was dead.

Now he thought about it again.

There is a hollowness in his stomach and his legs shake but he can name the reason and the boy, the new boy all gold and silver, moves in his mind again along the moonlight, his hair dampened by the lakewater into a dark animal sleekness, the eyes averted, knowing eyes, the flash of knee, the wet torso, the revealed sex.

The lake stretches out with its path of moonlight to where the loons utter their laments. There is a pull in the force of the water, the great mass of it pulling, an urging back to the source. Suicides often give in to its seduction. He could walk slowly, going always deeper and deeper until the water is over his head. Breath would be held for two minutes, life force fighting the water force, life force even when the conscious desire is death. The mass of water pounding in his ears like the muted roar of the sea in the vanilla and pink shell that Mrs. Carey kept on her tea table. The release of air, the replacement of air with water.

When Christ walked on the water, was he trying to walk into it? Was his tidal blood pulled by some different moon than the one that regulates the common ebb and flow? With his eyes, did he caress John's curls along John's cheeks, the folds of ear, the shadowed place underneath the jaw line, the gentle sweep of throat?

That would be one on God, as Malcolm would say. We got to face it, old man. God's done some bungling. Now, I'm willing to admit it. Digestive systems and mosquitoes and bad music, for Christ's sake. And everything rotting. Sure, new stuff growing but just so it can rot. What's the point? Malcolm's thoughts always came out of his mouth.

In his own bed, he had lain awake in the dark, his thoughts inchoate, a stone in his chest. The universe stretched off past spinning planets and blazing stars for as far as the mind could reach and when the mind reached the edge there was always the beyond, what was beyond the edge. Infinity ran its inky cloak against his thoughts and he could feel the brush of its passing and the folds falling back again, enclosing, smothering, retreating. And why was he in his bed in a provincial music college in a small prairie city, unable to sleep, his mind stretched toward some desire to know, his penis stretched and aching for the release of seed—all desire, mind and cock? Something made the mind, something made the phallus, something made the connections.

And were there right connections and wrong connections? What he would not allow himself to believe was that the disorder of his nerves, the mindless rushing of blood was connected to the slant of Malcolm's cheekbone in the dim light from the window, the small hollow at the base of his throat, the slender hand with its cigarette burned low. Malcolm went away to the coast when he was nineteen and died twenty years later in a Vancouver hospital from complications of tuberculosis that had been too often neglected. He had written five letters, the last wrapped around that street photograph with its light and shadow unconsciously recording the death that was coming soon: the cheekbones more prominent, a strand of hair escaping beneath his hat, the full mouth looking like it was ready to burst open again with its short, sharp inward laughter. "I'm often mistaken for Gregory Peck."

There were other Malcolms, he realizes now, brief Malcolms, but what did it matter? He only registered the feelings within himself, keeping them there like a rheumatism of the soul: a teacher one year with ready laughter and dark, straight hair who sang in the choir; a piano student with a cracking voice and the finest blonde fur forming along his cheeks, who played with a kind of passion that might have gone somewhere if he had ever practiced; a waiter at the legion. . . .

The Dejarlais boy.

Carroway?

The loons call again. Moon birds. And the moon connected to the blood cycles of women, but also to madness. Well, he is starting to know his own madness. Maybe this is something that happens after a first death. Such desperation to be like other people. The sad, trite initiation with the whore, his cock hard but unyielding. So important that at least he had put it where it was supposed to go. Everything in its place. A place to die, the lake, with night holding death's potency as lover holds lover's flesh. The lake drinking in the darkness, swallowing the water-bloated, embracing boys, urging them to dance, suspended, like marionettes. You are the best dancer, Jack, the young woman who nursed his mother tells him. And he is good: it's a natural talent like being able to coax Schuman's *Traumerei* out of the decrepit piano at the Churchill Lounge. For a while he wishes he might make all the expected moves— but he shies away; is pulled away. He quits going to dances. In the dark, alone, his legs thresh, he gasps for air, easing himself into night and sleep.

NINE

In the morning lake, he forces himself to swim, to put his body into that same water of the moon and the night. He has the lake all to himself, except for a sandpiper wandering along the beach. The sun is beneficent, as good as a landscape by Corot, he thinks, and smiles inwardly because the 'good as' comparison is something he hasn't thought of for months, maybe years. It was something Malcolm started when they first shared a room. Your cologne, he had said, is as good as a Packard 6-40 runabout. They racked their brains to see who could outdo the other. This weekend is as good as a wisecrack by Dorothy Parker. This sunset is as good as the *andante comodo* from Mahler's 9th Symphony. In that last letter that he had received just after the war, Malcolm had written, "I have finally found *the* perfect companion for me. She's as good as Glenfiddich Scotch. No, that's not it— she's as good as Ella Fitzgerald singing *For Sentimental Reasons*." Typical of Malcolm, he had forgotten to mention her name.

That last time he saw Malcolm, it had been a summer of similar heat, temperatures that turned the streets of the city into tepid passageways with people moving in slow motion, a film that has gone off its time. If anything, Malcolm had become thinner in the two months since they had graduated from college, a summer suit falling in loose folds from the point of a shoulder, a hip. About a block from the train station, he had broken into an impromptu tap dance, flashing his wing-tipped shoes, laughing at them. What do you think of these? As good as Theda Bara's eyebrows? A special sound to his laughter mixing with the tired drone of traffic, a fretful child somewhere. From a distance, they could hear the shouts of children playing a game, bickering.

The camp is beginning to stir. By the time Bragge and McEvoy have the teams sorted on the baseball diamond, the heat has come back and burned away the night moisture. The group assigned to him brandishes lavender-coloured ribbons. For Sports Day the population of the camp has been mixed to create even teams. From North Cabin there are only Carroway and Wesley with lavender markers. Carroway is sullen and tired, a white sailor's cap pulled over his forehead. Wesley squints into the sun, cleans his teeth with a finger.

"Now listen up," Frank Tupper hollers into a loud-haler. "Do we have a great day?"

The response is feeble.

"No. Let's really hear it. Do we have a great day for Sports Day or not?"

The cheers are louder. Carroway presses two fingers to a temple and massages. Tupper balances up and down on his toes, flashing sunlight from his whistle. "The Lord has blessed us and He expects everybody to do his best for his team. Now let's get things rolling, and to get things rolling we are going to have a half-hour scavenger hunt. Each of your group leaders has been given an envelope."

Fatigue has come back along with the heat. It had been impossible to sleep when he did get back to bed although, by then, all of the boys were back in their cots and even, when he checked, Carroway had succumbed, his damp hair stranded onto a pillow. He had thought of reading, but was afraid the light would awaken the boys. So he lay in the dark that moved slowly into morning greyness and his mind wandered along the old classrooms of the conservatory, through the Churchill Lounge at the Legion Hall, over the fields of the acreage. People were with him. He was alone. The ghosts came singly; they came in groups; they left him to his thoughts. He found himself accepting images that must have lain in some amphibious winter sleep, finally now to stir, thrusting the cold limbs of their life against the encasing mud. He did not resist them: he let his hand rest on the hand of the smiling teacher; he curled in the arms of the waiter, giving himself, drifting.

Wesley is standing in front of him and has said something. "We need the envelope," he repeats.

Yes, the envelope. It is in his shirt pocket. He opens it and pulls out the slips of paper. On the first is written: "Something with eyes that cannot see." On the next: "Something with legs that cannot run." Carroway who has come up next to him, is standing by his elbow repeating the phrases. The soft laugh has come back. "Something with a tongue that cannot speak."

They scatter with the papers.

The leaders meet at the picnic table. Mrs. Steinhauer has brought out coffee and doughnuts. Adeline is in her sports togs and a sun rash has already dusted her exposed shoulders with red. Frank Tupper's lips are powdered with icing sugar from the doughnut he is eating before the tray is even on the table.

Tiny seed pearls of moisture had lain along Malcolm's upper lip in the heat of the train station. The details have always been with him, the dots along the upper lip and, higher, tracing the hairline, the restless eyes coming back every few seconds to register his presence. God, you actually made it. What'd you tell the old lady? No, let me guess. You told her it was essential you come in and stock up on choir music for the coming winter. Something to quicken the hearts of matrons grown weary of *The Holy City*? New piano books for the kiddies you'll be teaching this fall. Such subterfuge, such goddamn plain, wonderful subterfuge, my son. Actually, his mother had said very little, hadn't she? If she had seen the letter Malcolm had sent suggesting they meet in the city for a couple of days while the exhibition was on, she made no reference to it. The set of her mouth had registered a touch of disapproval before it had lapsed into a kind of placid absolution. Boys must be boys. Young men must go off and do the things that young men do. She even gave him some money. Her hands had fluttered around his collar and tie, adjusting, patting, finding an offending bit of lint on his shoulder, and then straying, for a second, to touch his cheek, softly, shyly, retreating to the pockets of her smock. He felt an urge to fold his arms around her but it was something he didn't do any more since he had grown big enough to fit into his father's clothing. Have a good time, she said, and he had watched her waving to him from the parlour window, the movement of her hand reminding him of a bird exploring the mystery of glass, the incomprehensible barriers.

She told me to have a good time.

Malcolm did a fake skid-stop, mouth open in a vaudeville *o* of surprise, his eyebrows prancing.

"Are you with us, Jack." The words come muffled through chews of doughnut. "We've got to thank Terry and Shirley for thinking all of those up last night." Stray icing is licked from blunt fingers.

Something is wrong with Shirley Stickles. Her eyes are puffy, red-rimmed, streaming. She refuses a doughnut. Something more than in her appearance though.

"I only set them down for a minute. I can't see how I could possibly have misplaced them."

Her glasses.

"You don't have another pair?" Adeline breaks off a piece of doughnut and inspects it as if it were somehow responsible.

"I wouldn't even have taken them off but Carroway thought I was getting an infection and he offered to go and get the mirror and I thought there was something starting. I am prone to styes."

"They couldn't have just disappeared."

One of the smaller boys, his lavender ribbon flying, dashes by the table shouting, "I got it. I got the first one." Waving a potato in his hand. Millie Steinhauer rolls her eyes upward. "God, what's happening to my kitchen! I can imagine."

They are silent except for McEvoy offering soft words of comfort to the distraught Shirley Stickles. Bragge finishes his coffee and lights a cigarette. Running boys crisscross the green with their trophies.

"You look tired, Jack." Adeline Tupper's fingers against his elbow. "We can put Burgess or MacDonald on your group if you want to take some time to rest."

"I am a bit tired."

They persuade him to go back to the cabin and lie down during the novelty races which will take until lunch. I'm not sure I should be letting you go off this year, Mrs. Washburne had muttered, fussing with her gift of rhubarb tarts. You never do remember about stopping for rests. Has she ever flung herself into the vortex of infinity or has life, for her, always been as circular and enclosed as a tart top? Three children working in the city, a husband with a distinguished war record. A witness to terrible things in her life, London bombed and burning, being uprooted from her homeland— yet everything somehow in its proper place. Had she ever looked into the black holes of space, the black holes of the heart? Had any one of the people he had known in his lifetime? Malcolm— maybe. Mrs. Carey?

Flower boy, she called him. Without derision. But she recognized him as someone different. Queer? Sometimes the words of abuse are most exact and right. They were both queer in different ways. There are other words of course. Fruit. Whoever thought of that one? Fecundity doesn't seem the right image. Maybe ripeness and softness. Had anyone ever thought him ripe and soft? Pansy. That was another one of the words. He actually didn't mind that one. His mother always had a bed of pansies underneath the pantry window. He seemed to remember her telling him it was from the French word *pensée*— because they looked like thinkers. Are thinkers queer? It is possible to go in circles, and, in fact, he is none of them and yet all of them.

Faggot. Burgess likes that one.

His eyes are burning. His fingertips can feel the heat along the socket rim. The skull: that is what he is feeling really— one of the bits of soft rock that will erode and turn into sand and maybe, in time, go whirling into the infinity of space. Odd to think of the bone under the skin. Everything, bone and skin and blood and mind from one fleck of sperm conjoined with one miniscule egg. The accidentalness of it. Generations lost when the connections are not made. Nature's way. The jewelweed bursts at a touch, hundreds of seeds flung out with nothing but the desire for life written in their atoms and only a few destined for germination.

If he could only sleep, maybe the burning across his eyes, along his forehead, would go away. The other ache, in his chest, along his arm, has become a part of him and it is only present with a kind of heavy dullness. If it refuses to go away, he will have to give up playing at the Legion entirely. Maybe a good thing; maybe it's time. But what is left? Accompanying the church choir which seems to be getting smaller every year along with the congregation. Continuing to take students, listening to their scales and Hanon exercises. *Albumblatt*. His life has become what Malcolm refused. A cigarette underlining his complaint. The mater, of course, wants me to come home and help her and the old man in the store, take it over eventually I suppose. Sell canned pears and gum boots and lead the choir practice on Wednesday nights. Christ, that's enough to put me to sleep forever.

Malcolm talked the whole time they made their way from the train station to his aunt's and uncle's house on the south side of the city. They detoured past the college, its windows flung open for air, a Chopin polonaise drifting over the grounds to the sidewalk. Malcolm muttering. Christ, we're lucky we never had to take summer school. The polonaise stopped abruptly in the middle of a phrase and, from one of the small gables set into the mansard roof, through another open window, a tenor voice sought the thick, unmoving air. *To still a heart in absence wrung: I tell each bead unto the end.* Oh fuck, Malcolm hooting. Dean Richard's wife ain't gonna give the old beads a rest. She's got some pimply kid singing *The Rosary* again. Then breaking into full voice and singing in unison with the disembodied voice: *O memories that bless and burn! O barren gain and bitter loss!* A baffled face appeared at the window. Malcolm waving and shouting. Keep a stiff upper vibrato, son. The pearls of moisture on his face collected and made small streams. His eyes were bright with excitement. There's a good chance I'm going to Vancouver, he confided. I need to go somewhere. And I can stay with Maude and Elmer to start with. You could too, I bet, if I asked them.

Malcolm's cousin, Maude, was angular and taut like Malcolm, chain-smoking, breaking into abrupt haws of laughter the way he did. He sensed an affinity between the two, an ability that siblings and cousins sometimes have to communicate through a look, the tip of a head, a hand gesture. Had he felt jealous of their closeness? Elmer, her husband, was a paunchy saxophone-player who already, in the early afternoon, had a glow on. He talked expansively of Vancouver, the wonderful weather, the better chance for jobs. Maude winked at Malcolm. An older couple, Maude's parents, were part of the porch group, and Maude's brother, a boy slightly younger than himself and Malcolm. Maude, teasingly, kept calling him Barrington. The boy's face was red with the heat of the afternoon, the excitement of the company, and he kept ducking his head and stuttering c-c-cut it out. Barrington was his name but he had truncated it to Barry.

Malcolm had been dead now for sixteen—seventeen?—years. Had he ever found anything better than canned pears and gum boots? Elmer's band is mostly a pipe dream, Barry had confided when he ran into him once in the city, three or four years after Malcolm had gone to the coast. Maude's left him, you know. Malcolm's been working the movie theatres—doing their singalong intermissions.

Another time, just before the war, he visited the Fairchild aunt and uncle and found out that Malcolm had taken day shifts in a plywood mill while he still played in a number of different dancebands in the evenings. When the band dates were sparse, he did gigs in some of the bars. Then he had written again. I've even been playing the piano in one of those dives that we used to think existed only in the movies. Lots of smoke and lowlife. I do a lot of faking on an upright that's seen better days. Scraps of words on letters in a biscuit tin, the way some people keep the ashes of the cremated.

There was some money put away now, from his work, from the sale of his mother's acreage. He should travel a bit. Go to Vancouver again. He had gone two summers after Malcolm died. Just after the war. His mother wanted to see the Rockies and Aunt Florence was living in Victoria so he drove her there. His first car, that would have been. A 1938 Studebaker. He drove her to Victoria and then went back to Vancouver for three days.

Three days out of the world. He lay on the beach at English Bay in his black wool swimsuit, his limbs chalk white. Families rested and ran in and out of the water and read and built things out of sand. Young women sunned. The burnished legs of young men flashed back and forth in front of him and sometimes they rested too, the young men, their bodies brown and oiled, and the ache of longing came over him. He had never been so alone. The sea swept out to big boats anchored against the horizon. At night the city lights, the ship lights, fell into the glass-still water. There was a smell of dampness and salt, a faintness of tar and burning sawdust.

One of the evenings he went to the Boston Nightspot on Hastings Street where Malcolm had played piano up until a few months before he died. It was small and dark and smoke-filled with a scarred piano over in one corner. A man who seemed to have no age was playing radio hits and slipping in a bit of Gershwin. Their eyes met in a kind of recognition, the kind of recognition that he had noticed between Maude and Malcolm on that summer afternoon, except here the kinship was a sexual brotherhood, a cousinship of men whose hearts are stirred by other men, and the questions he had of Malcolm remained unsaid and he looked away, quickly finished his beer and went back to his hotel. In memory of Malcolm, he smoked until the darkness of the night began its diffusion into a new day.

One of the boys has come in. Potherby. His face flushed, pulling up his sweatsocks.

"How is it going?" Forcing himself to his feet, his hands against the curtains for steadiness.

"The greens won the wheelbarrow and the yellows won the sack race. Our team won the egg-and-spoon though. Mrs. Tupper says to tell you lunch is ready." Potherby hops from one foot to the other.

"You run along. I'll be up in a minute."

In the hall, Mrs. Steinhauer is dishing out baked beans.

"I feel as if I've been working like a farmer all morning," says Frank Tupper, and then, hollering at Mrs. Steinhauer, "Hope you made enough for threshers, Millie. That used to be something, eh, cooking for the threshing crew."

At the next table, Burgess and MacDonald are chanting: "Beans, beans, the musical fruit."

Mrs. Steinhauer has ladled an extra large portion for him before he can stop her. The beans have been cooked to a rust-coloured mash. Out of the corner of his eye, he can see Burgess has taken a spoonful and is pretending he has been poisoned, grasping his stomach with both hands, groaning. Terry McEvoy waves his fork at the boys' table. "Burgess, if you're going to die, get it over with quickly so the rest of us can enjoy our meal." He smiles at Millie Steinhauer who has finally eased into a place herself and seems to be eyeing her own dish rather dubiously.

"Did you get a bit of shut-eye?" says Adeline. Whatever she had on her plate has disappeared.

"Not really sleep. Some rest."

"That's good."

"Missed a great race." Tupper cleans his plate with the last of his dinner roll. "You should've seen the three-legged race. Cardinal ended up with that chunky little red-headed kid from West Cabin. Talk about comic relief."

"I thought the funniest thing was that Wesley from your cabin, Jack, being the wheelbarrow with Carroway driving. I've never seen hands move so fast. I think Carroway must have threatened him with something like murder." McEvoy chuckles.

"Where is Carroway?" Shirley Stickles, still without glasses, squints at the other tables.

"Ate his lunch in three minutes flat," says Adeline Tupper, "and then announced he had some things to get ready for their skit tonight."

An ebb and flow of noise in the hall: dishes being scraped, the piping voices of the younger children, the odd deepness and changes of pitch of those into puberty, chairs scraping the plywood floor, giggling. It seems to go beyond time. Flystrips coil from the ceiling where the heat is trapped, suffused and radiating. His clothes are damp again.

The elements— the trapped heat, the coils of flypaper, clothing sticking to the body— they return from that last supper with Malcolm, his aunt frying chicken, all of them talking and laughing too loud from the beers they have consumed throughout the afternoon. Malcolm's excitement had grown. He couldn't sit still for longer than five minutes, pacing around the kitchen, chewing on a drumstick, checking photographs on a bureau, smoking, always smoking.

Little Johnny Hislop, he announced to the kitchen assembly. The world's greatest room mate. Give him a pat on the back, Maudie, or a kiss on the cheek—though he'll blush for a week. Laughing at the sudden rhyme. Naw, I mean it. Kept this bad actor on the straight and narrow; kept him off the paths of temptation. Now the question, of course—would he know a path of temptation if he saw one?

There is a scraping of chairs. The meal is finished and they move outside into the sun's glare, the wash of heat.

The afternoon is to be a round robin softball tournament with adults portioned onto teams. Adeline Tupper has borrowed one of the children's ball-gloves and practices jumping up, her gloved hand extended as if she is catching flies.

"Way to go, Mrs. Tupper," MacDonald shouts, and then in a whisper to Burgess and Cardinal, "If she ends up on base, I'm going to do some sliding in. See if I can bump into a bit of tit."

"Christ, how could you *not* run into it." Cardinal's observation. "Too bad Metro isn't here."

"Do you feel up to umping, Jack?" Frank Tupper speaking through a mangled catcher's mask, not waiting for an answer, sprinting over to his position in front of the chicken-wire backstop. "Alright, listen up. The first teams on are the Falcons and the Magpies and the winners will play the Pelicans."

He stands behind the catcher to make the calls. The sky has become almost white with heat and the dust from the base-runners hangs suspended along the diamond. Tupper is catching Cardinal's pitches. His mouth never stops: "Way-to-go, Chief. Burn 'em in here. They won't even see it coming. We got a sucker here and I mean a ten-cent all day sucker. Just out here to lick. Attaboy, Card." Like a carnival barker. The loud, mindless shouts of the barkers had mingled with the jittery carnival music when he and Malcolm had gone with Maude and Elmer and Barry, along with the aunt and uncle, to the exhibition after supper. They had grouped themselves with Elmer and Maude's parents in one little cluster, stopping at each booth to gamble or try their skill with darts and popguns and tossed coins. Maude had linked arms with Malcolm. The two of them, Malcolm in his suit the colour of vanilla ice-cream, his wing-tipped shoes, Maude in a dress that she had changed into for the evening, something with a satin-like sheen that latticed across her breasts and hugged her thin hips and flared out around her ankles, in high-heeled shoes that were almost impossible to walk in, a glittery clip in her hair the same auburn colour as her cousin's. As they coursed along the midway, people stopped to stare at them, these two creatures who seemed to shine with the night and the carnival lights, insular, laughing at something the rest of the world couldn't see. He had paired up awkwardly with Barry. Years later, Barry disappeared, one of the many unaccounted for when the war was over and the boys came home. Auntie Peggy believes he will still show up, Malcolm had written in one of his five letters. She thinks he must have been shellshocked and lost his memory like Ronald Coleman in that movie I guess.

It is important to concentrate. The afternoon seems endless. Burgess's Magpies cannot be put out. The other boys lose interest in the game Bowmeister and Potherby are making dandelion chains in their field positions. A hawk cries overhead, piercing, sudden, and then hovers in silence. The fat boy has settled himself, like a sad Eastern god, against the backstop. In their journey along the midway, they had gone, hadn't they, to one of the sideshow tents to see the fat man with his cascading folds of flesh, and, in another tent, they watched a hermaphrodite with full breasts and male genitals who stroked himself as he sang *If I were the only girl in the world and* . . . (with a little moue of surprise) *I* . . . *were the only boy* . . . , his lips rouged, his teeth yellow. Maude and Malcolm clutching each other with helpless laughter. As they made their way to the exit, Elmer, in a last stand, drunkenly flinging a baseball at a pyramid of dumbells, shouting as they collapsed. Hey, Maudie, won you a little kewpie doll here. Whaddaya think of that? I don't need it, Maude giggling, give it to Barrington.

He had never been much of a ball player although his grade six teacher, he remembers, had tried to encourage him. You're a good runner, Jackie. You've just got to learn to hit the ball. It was true. When he did hit the ball, he ran like a person possessed, ran until his whole body seemed to be one gasping pain. Once he hit a home run, a grounder into left field, and because he ran the bases too quickly, the whole world whirling and blurring, he ended up staggering over behind the school building and heaving into the nettles there, a pain stabbing through his side.

"What was that call, Jack?" Tupper has whipped off his mask. His face is red and streaked with grime.

He's missed it, missed the play. There is a moment's silence all along the playing field. "I'm sorry. Maybe somebody else had better take a turn umping."

"Aw, shit." Cardinal throws down his glove and turns his back on him from the pitcher's mound.

"Well, I'll call that one," Tupper shouts. "That was a strike if I ever saw one. Clean and straight over the plate. You're out, Charlie."

The batter, one of the younger boys, doesn't seem very concerned. Something he expected.

"That's not fair." Burgess screaming. "Only an ump can call a play."

Terry McEvoy's hand on his shoulder. "I'll take over for a while, Jack. My team won't be on 'til later."

"At least this one's got eyes," Burgess mutters.

Heading back toward the compound, he can feel the shaking in his arms, his legs. Too much standing. He should have said no to start with. At the parking lot, the black '51 Ford glimmers under its fine coating of dust pocked with last night's rain. His hands open the door and there is a rush of escaping heat. In the glove compartment, behind all the papers, behind the pill bottles, there is a package of Players. The cellophane is insistent but it finally crackles off. The smoke he draws in seems to smooth the shuddering. He is sitting in the passenger seat, where the Dejarlais boy sat on their trip to Grace Lake. Smiling. Shy to talk. And so he talked to him, hadn't he? Talked to cover the strange, suppressed excitement that was in himself the whole time, body and nerves reacting to some mindless connection. Giving the friendly neighbour smile, an uncle's words: How did you get along at school this year, Roy? Is your dad still working with the section crew?

And then the boy stretched out on the grass, after they had eaten sandwiches by the Carey place. And took his shirt off so that the sun soaked into his skin and became his skin and there were soft tufts of new hair dark in his armpits and sweat pooled and glistened in his navel. And, for a minute or two, the boy slept while he watched, shaken, his hands anchored in his pockets or busy with a cigarette. His blood was crazy. Mr. Carey's larkspurs bloomed within eyesight, although the old man himself was long dead, his hands frozen to the steering wheel of the Plymouth halfway into Whittier's barn. What had Mrs. Carey said when they got her out and she stood looking at the car burrowing into the old barnwood? That isn't where it goes. She began laughing so hard she couldn't stop and someone looked in her purse to see if she had any medication with her and inside there was a dead bird, a sparrow, and some withered stalks of bleeding heart. She became a story that was told, for a while.

TEN

On the seventh day, the day stranded midway between the arrival and the departure of the boys, John Hislop makes his way outside the North Cabin in the early evening, standing for a moment as if he has forgotten why he has come out, why he has set aside his pressing book, the old dictionary in which fresh petals sweat their colours into strange words. It is only a moment, of course, and he remembers that Drama Night is beginning, a night that has in the past taken on characteristics of those festivals that rub perfunctorily against religion and then steal off for a good

time. The costumes might have come from Hal-
loween cast-offs. Mardi Gras ribaldry peppers the
air.

Even the restraining wrap of this year's Bibli-
cal theme cannot totally dampen the boys'
enthusiasm. He hears the evening humming, sees
the dashing of strangely garbed figures across the
compound. Somehow, he is aware of details in a
way that he has never known before. Each blade
of grass has definition, a stalk of fireweed shim-
mers, multiflorous, each blossom holding to its
own variation of milk-pinks and magentas. He
has a sense of having taken a long time to walk
up the incline to the mess hall but if anyone asks
him, he cannot say whether it has taken him five
minutes or twenty-five.

Inside the hall, tables are collapsed and
stacked against the walls and chairs range the
floor in concentric semi-circles. Mrs. Steinhauer
waves him to a chair that she has saved. There is
an odd sense of activity, of people moving with
destinations and purposes that somehow do not
align, delaying the start of the show. In a matter
of minutes, Mrs. Steinhauer is snoring softly. The
sound rubs against him and he hears it from
another time. In the small bungalow, he and Malcolm had shared Barry's bedroom, the cousins
falling asleep on the bed while he made a nest
out of a quilt on the floor. But he had reached a
point past exhaustion and sleep eluded him.
Already a touch of dawn crept into the room and
he could feel the closeness of the sleeping figures,

sense the heat of their bodies, Barry with his arms and legs outflung, the limbs boyishly smooth but a thatching of soft hair in the armpit, a few curled in the hollow of his chest. Listening to the soft snoring, he finally gave in to sleep and, when he opened his eyes, Malcolm was already awake, sitting up in bed, smoking. Barry remained dead to the world but his morning erection waved freely out from his underwear. Christ, will you look at that lollipop, Malcolm chortled. He could feel his face flame the colour of Barry's questing gland, feel a weakness engulf his body. From the dresser top where Barry had left it, Malcolm grabbed the bamboo cane with the kewpie doll clasping it and began brushing the kewpie's feathered dress against Barry's exposure, singing softly in a simpering imitation of Helen Kane. *Give me a little kiss, will ya huh.* Barry began thrusting into the air and then, with a gasp, shot his load. Malcolm had become hysterical with laughter in the process, nearly falling off the bed and, as Barry threshed his way out of the dream to consciousness, Maude flung open the bedroom door. What the hell's going on in here? No one can sleep. Seeing Barry, she screamed and retreated as they grabbed for blankets. Don't worry about Maude, Malcolm had chuckled. I told you about when I was fifteen and three months, didn't I?

Tupper is poised on the wooden risers that have been dragged forward to create a stage. One of the yard lights which has been rigged up inside picks up the shiny spots on his balding forehead. He speaks into a microphone that squeals every few seconds, sending Terry McEvoy scurrying to fiddle with the controls on an amplifier. With the clearing of his throat amplified into the hall, there is a settling, an easing of flesh against the wood of chairs. At a point of optimum stillness, the minister's voice rolls across the room: "It was Shakespeare who said 'the play's the thing'. Well we say 'the play's the thing and the Bible is the book' and tonight the play is the Bible. This year our Drama Night is very special because all of the skits—we can thank Miss Stickles for coming up with the idea—are based on dramatic incidents from the Holy Scriptures." Shirley Stickles, her eyes still red and streaming, smiles weakly and nods. "We are reminded that within the Bible, the received word of God, are some of the greatest stories, stories of the conflict of good and evil."

Tupper's voice has become sonorous and self-perpetuating. There is a scurry of activity from the staffroom off to the side of the platform. Adeline is visible for a minute, shooing a small boy in a bathing suit covered with wild rhubarb leaves onto stage. Tupper adjusts the microphone downwards and there is another squeal of the machine that brings hands to ears. Millie Steinhauer snorts awake.

"My name is Adam." The small boy's voice comes gravelly, softly into the microphone which picks up his breathing as much as what he is saying. "I am the first man in the world and God has given me the job of naming all the animals. 'Cat' was easy but 'hippopotamus' . . . "

It is still light outside, but the high windows of the hall reveal a softening, an acceptance of the dusk. The spotlight seems to grow brighter as the play progresses. Adam shines. God enters with a cottonball beard, waving a weather-bleached rib bone which he hides behind his back as Adeline ushers on a rather bewildered Eve, layered in wild rhubarb and sporting a rag-mop wig. A titter of laughter ripples through the crowd. Eve scowls.

The side doors of the hall are open but the building is even hotter than it has been all day. The crease on his last pair of clean trousers has wilted. Dampness is spreading in a circle from each armpit. A snake with green crêpe paper scales bleeding verdure across naked limbs and torso is onstage hissing his s's, tempting Eve with a green apple.

Paradise is lost again. The stains of knowledge begin to set. Adam the labeller adds new words to his vocabulary. Shame. Guilt. In the instant of leaving Eden, he pauses and looks back, the snake boy, body asserting itself through the limp, leeching scales.

The audience breaks into applause. His North Cabin boys are leaving their seats and heading for the staffroom door. Tupper has wrestled the microphone, squealing protests, back to his mouth. "Let's hear it for the Garden of Eden."

Everyone claps again. And then they applaud the cast who shuffle back out in wilted leaves and seeping crêpe paper. There is another hand for Mrs. Tupper who supervised it all. The sound of palm smacking against palm; the movement of hands stirring the heat. "While the stagehands are setting up for our next item on the agenda, I will take the time to tell you. . . . " Tupper's voice drifts over the restlessness in the hall. It is soothing, hypnotic. When he closes his eyes, Malcolm is waiting, sitting across from him at a varnished table scarred with carved initials and cigarette burns in a cafe that had been a hangout for the college students. They had two hours before he had to catch the train home. The afternoon sunlight came in through the cafe window, framing him, lighting fire along the edge of his hair. His face had the pallor of a figure in a Holman Hunt painting, a pallor that was underpainted so that it seemed to glow. The light of the world. He was quieter than usual. I think I'm going back with Elmer and Maude, he said. Elmer says they need a good vocalist, had me sing some pop songs for him. I did my Rudy Vallee imitation. Elmer was impressed. He lit a cigarette elaborately, giving the pronouncement time to settle over the table. So what do you think? Smoke diffused the contours of his face. It was like he was disappearing already. You should come too, old man, another of Malcolm's phrases, old man, as if he lived in a movie or a novel where people had dinner jackets and butlers. There's always work for a good pianist. Even if the band business doesn't work out, there's always the churches. We could make enough to live, go to the beach on our time off. Maudie says it's a great life. The winters are a lot easier.

It was something he had thought about on the train ride home and in the days afterward, his mind filled with a kind of unfocused longing, a yearning for Malcolm, for young people, for a different place. What's troubling you, his mother asked him a few days later. She was setting out bone china cups for a tea, a meeting of the church ladies, wiping each cup and saucer with a tea towel, admiring the individual patterns, arranging them on a sideboard in the small parlour. You haven't been the same since you got back from the city. Is something wrong? He told her about the invitation offhandedly, as if it were something to which he wouldn't give a serious thought. The parlour curtains allowed sunlight in, sunlight with a greenish cast and, through the exposed glass between the cloth panels, he could see a small patch of Ferble's Lake, Mirror Lake, in the distance, at the bottom of the sloping orchard. There was a quiet, secret space between the curtain and the window. As a boy, he had often hidden there. With the drapery behind him, he could catch the reflection of his face, a transparency of himself, the small, pointed, pale face of a rheumatic child, elusive, shifting, becoming the trees, the shining patch of lake, the far sky. From a maroon-covered set of children's encyclopedias, his mother read him the story of Narcissus and he thought of it often, hidden in the curtain folds, watching his face in the window, the face moving as he moved, turning when he turned. He would ask her to read it again. The story of the boy turned into a flower; the face transfixed by its own image, peering into the lake. Mirror Lake. Perhaps this was to be his only ocean, this bit of water blazing white against the poplars and willows.

Sometimes, with his back against the window, his shoulder blades pressed against the sill, he would watch her through the loosely-woven drapery. Often she would forget he was there. She would move from the piano to the wooden secretary with its glass door to a basket with her sewing, lost in thought, her hands moving objects carefully into alignments charted in her mind, a photograph at a certain angle, a book in a particular spot, cloth folded and refolded.

A cup fell and bone china lay scattered over the parlour floor. He picked up the shards, one with a perfect painted rose on it. His mother was weeping quietly. Your father gave me that cup. She held the bereft saucer. It was for our anniversary. You were just born. He helped her to her bedroom to lie down, promised to finish getting the tea ready. Her hand grabbed hold of his as he turned to leave the room. I'll die, she whispered. If you leave, I'll die.

You could come too.

I'll die, she said.

Tupper's voice has stopped and the room is filled with an expectant hush. "And now," the voice revives, "I'm glad to see Mr. Hislop sitting front-row-centre because the boys of North Cabin have been working especially hard on their skit." He squints at his notes. "And the skit is called 'Happy Birthday, Herod' so let's hear it for the North Cabin Players."

Potherby scuttles out from the staffroom door in a bathrobe. He has a red bandana rolled and tied around his forehead. At the side of the platform, he turns on a record player. Carroway's record player. One of Carroway's rock and roll records bursts into sound: instrumental, loud, with a thudding bass and a manic piano. Potherby ups the volume for a minute; the floodlight is clicked off and then, as it is turned on again, the volume is turned gradually down, fading into the heat and the moth-dotted lambency of the stage.

Adeline has come from the staffroom and settled into the chair vacant at his other side. "Lord what a racket," she says. "Herod must be turning in his grave."

Potherby goes up to the microphone and stands on tiptoe to speak into it. "Our story," his voice squeaks and then finds a register, "takes place in the court of King Herod. King Herod spends most of his time worrying about people trying to steal his crown from him. The Romans only let him do some of the ruling and now there's stories going around that there's a new king of the Jews in the land. Even though it's his birthday party, he's having trouble getting cheered up."

Burgess and MacDonald come onstage in makeshift togas, bearing chairs which they cover with blankets. They are clumsy and self-conscious, carbon copies of a hundred boys who have camped at Grace Lake over the years. That's all Dejarlais should have been: an awkward adolescent, playing ball, running to the lake, forgetting his lines in the Drama Night skits. Why was he singled out? Some force moving him into the car seat, burning him against the bedsheet, sucking his life into the muskeg. The wild, trapped-animal eye, terror-ridden. But it doesn't see him; it sees the body dissolving into sand, shifting atoms that are only held in their configuration within the moment of the spirit. A touch will disassemble them, send them whirling into space, into the void. The light from the windows has grown dimmer, the heat, if possible, more humid and pressing.

Wesley and Bowmeister have replaced Potherby at the microphone. Wesley is wearing a purple car-robe and a tinfoil crown. Bowmeister is beside him, his mouth grotesquely lipsticked, a tea towel over his head, a pillow stuffed into a bathrobe for a bosom.

Adeline's elbow nudges him. "I think my

earrings look better on Bowmeister than they do on me."

"Happy birthday, my dear," Bowmeister speaks in a high falsetto.

"It cannot be otherwise," Wesley talks huskily into the microphone, "with you at my side, my radiant queen."

Potherby comes in and kneels before them. "Pardon me, my lord. Great news!"

"Rise and speak."

"The heretic John they call the Baptist has been captured as you commanded."

Carroway has written the script. But where is Carroway?

"We bring him to you as a birthday offering."

Cardinal, bound with ropes, is brought onstage by MacDonald and Burgess. He is dressed in torn gunny sacks belted with more rope. His hair has been carefully slicked back and he is wearing black, horn-rimmed glasses. Shirley Stickles' glasses. His glasses.

Adeline's mouth falls open. "What?"

As if from a distance, he can see himself, the old man on the chair, trying to move forward, trying to rise. There is no strength. Burgess is carrying a spear. He can feel its point going into his chest, the pain spreading like flower petals, a pain almost comforting in its radiance.

"In the eyes of the Lord," shouts Cardinal, "you have sinned." The second spear thrust. The pain is powerful, a sunburst. Sparks fly to his shoulder, tingle along his arm. "May the Lord have pity on you for you have sinned grievously."

"Take him away," Wesley grunts.

"Blaspheming scum," screeches Bowmeister through his wound of lipstick.

"Still, they call him prophet and messiah."

"Do not be upset, my dearest." Bowmeister toys with a lock of Wesley's hair. "Put him out of your mind. My daughter Salome has prepared a special dance in honour of your birthday."

The two retreat to their prepared chairs. Potherby scuttles out again to the record player. He turns it on full volume. The bass throbs, the piano climbs and then crashes and then climbs again like waves breaking against a beach. From time to time there is a high-pitched screaming that ties in with the crescendo. Electric guitars pulsate.

The pain is coming in waves, rising in his throat, bilious and insistent. His legs cannot move. He gasps and gasps again for air.

At a climax of the noise, Carroway leaps onto the stage. He is a swirl of sheets and toweling and tinfoil jewellery. He lowers his draped arm to reveal the painted face, the fleshy blood-circle of lips, rouged cheeks, eyes outlined in mascara, rimmed with turquoise. As he dances, he sheds the towels, the sheets, until he is finally whirling naked around the stage except for a swim suit cupping his genitals in filigrees of tinfoil. The music thunders to a stop. He drops prostrate before the fat boy, lying still except for the sucking in and the heaving out of air, the involuntary movement of the stomach, the twitch of an ankleted foot remembering in a small spasm the dance.

Beside him, Mrs. Steinhauer groans. It is impossible to move. He is rivetted with pain: if he moves he will shatter, break into shards of bone. His mouth is open, trying to say something, trying to cry out but there is no sound.

"Splendid! What beauty!" Wesley simpers. "You shall have whatever wish is closest to your heart. Ask, and it shall be granted."

Has his own voice called out "No!" or has it only exploded inside his head?

Carroway rises, silver and gold in the floodlight. "I have but one desire, my lord. I ask that the head of John the Baptist be brought to me upon a serving tray." The red circle of lips, the smile of the anemone.

"It shall be done," grins the fat boy.

He is able to force himself part way out of his chair. He is almost standing. Cardinal screams offstage, a cry of horror, a death cry. "Don't touch me! Don't touch me!" And the cry is in his own throat, choking him. Burgess comes in carrying a skillet against the flat of his upended palm. On it is the head, pale, angular, thinning hair, mouth caught open. Crude, but a close enough approximation in papier-mâché. Black horn-rimmed glasses. He hears a woman's voice somewhere crying.

It is the last sound, growing into a roar, the thunder of water in his ears and when he closes his eyes there is the enfolding black redness that sends him whirling down downwards twin boys drifting with him the hours I spent with thee OGodOgodOgod the jewelweed bursting milkweed seeds trailing from broken pods on silver strands in green curtains cool against his cheeks on rhubarb tarts the wasps drink silently the sky falls into the lake.

E L E V E N

They drove by night, speeding in the darkness along the paved highway. There was a minute in that whole journey when John Hislop felt consciousness burst through a corolla of numbness to a blaze of pain. He grabbed hold of the pain for that minute, to register the world, the sense of being contained but moving, hurtling forward, someone holding his hand, someone— a woman, the hand slender, the hand and arm extended from a form somewhere else. Where? From the other side of a car seat? Where is he lying? He is allowed the minute before the next wave and, when it comes, he doesn't resist, drifting into it, feeling the force drawing him back and down. Under.

Whether it is hours or days before he again opens his eyes, he is not certain. He tries to ask the nurse but the words come out aborted, deformed from the side of his mouth. He stops them with a laugh that sounds to his ears pathetic, gurgling, closer to a cough. You're right, Malcolm, I can't laugh, never could, never will.

But once the nurse has pushed a needle into his hip he finds Malcolm waiting, waiting and serious, although there is a tremulousness to the edge of the lips, a twitching that can give way to abrupt laughter.

Well, old man, this is it. He does laugh then, just a snort, as he pulls up the collar of his Gregory Peck raincoat.

It is raining in the cemetery. A funeral in the rain: the mind seeks the comfortable stage settings. A gentle, general rain, earth and sky meeting in water, water streaming from the roofs, the shingled slant of his own house and the Washburne house down the street, the flat, tar-rimmed hospital roof, the slated steeple of the Anglican church turning black, the roof of the Legion Hall weeping onto the dandelions below. The rain seeps along the contours of the Dejarlais house and stains the ill-fitting coat of the woman making her way down the path, through a gateless opening to a board sidewalk. Drops of rain pearl on her flat cheeks, on her sleek, black purse. She would come, of course, joining the group at the graveside. There had been an acknowledged kinship, hadn't there? The family of those who do not fit.

Malcolm in his Gregory Peck raincoat, his eyes burning like soft interior fires against the damp. He supports the arm of Mrs. Carey, Mrs. Carey in a long winter coat and a Queen Mary hat with blossoms tangled in its net. Larkspur. Her mouth trembles, verging on laughter, tears, a pronouncement? Flower boy. Malcolm winks at him, fishes a cigarette package from his pocket, gently releases the limb of the old woman to perform the complex task of lighting it in the rain. Soon, old man, he whispers. Soon.

The words are absorbed by the rain washing the casket, the mounded earth, the mourners assembled in a magnet shape around the oblong pit. Adeline Tupper and Shirley Stickles have covered their heads with plastic kerchiefs. Mrs. Washburne is the only one present with an umbrella, an alien, exotic touch. A group of women radiate out from the umbrella spokes, faces quick and stolid, townswomen who gravitate to gravesides as they do to whist drives, their fingers clutching purses, eyes alert for any crack in the conformity of ritual, something to savour over coffee later. Are they blind to Malcolm, to Mrs. Carey, the Indian woman?

Soon, old man, Malcolm whispers, the whisper ending with a chuckle, a rasping, smoker's chuckle that turns into a cough. And then he is singing oh so softly, *the hours I spent with thee, dear heart, are like a string of pearls to me.* There is a longing in his own clay fingers to trace the high cheekbone, push back the loose strand of hair, brush against the lips, stop the silly words. *I count them over every one apart. My rosary, my rosary.* Malcolm's singing grows fainter. He hums a forgotten line, his lean face aslant the music, head cocked as if the words might come from some hidden prompter. *To still a heart in absence wrung.* Ah, yes. Laughing. Singing the line again strongly with a calculated catch in his voice. Winking at him. That should make Dean Richards' wife wet her pants.

Who was at your graveside, Malcolm? Musicians, forlorn without their music, a woman remembering how it felt to wrap her legs around thin, taut thighs and smell the smoke breath and hear the little death cries of released love. The tear-salt wind moving toward the mountain all covered with snow. Did I, Malcolm, did I court too slow?

In the yard filled with bones, the Indian woman leaves the gathering to pull weeds off the boy's plot. Is that why she has really come? She returns to the mourners, her hands filled with yarrow and lamb's quarter and crumpled crabgrass. Once their hands had touched and he felt a sympathy, yes for the lost boy, but for something else too. Perhaps a sympathy for pain that ran parallel in their lives like rail steel.

Tracks on ties dipped against the elements in a similar pitch. She will not go back for coffee with the clustered women. What does she remember in the rain? That other coffin being lowered, what it felt like to push the child from her body in the release of birth, the ease of pain, the touch of a small hand reaching out for ginger snaps, a halting voice recalling a picture show? Or does she remember him, the man who took her boy to Grace Lake? Ferry man. Fairy man.

Soon, Malcolm whispers. His lips have quit singing, his large liquid eyes are fixed on the casket moving into the grave.

He sleeps and the pain is gone. When he wakes, it is night and the tattoo of the rain has stopped. His eyes have become friendly with the dark, finding corners where a ceiling meets a wall, finding a rectangle of window and its hint of a soft, clouded sky beyond, finding the metal piping at the foot of a bed. In a matter of time he might be able to make out the figure sitting in the most shadowed corner of the room.

Soon, it whispers.

He remembers the flowers mounded over the earth as the mourners drifted away. Among the carnations and roses were Adeline's wild tiger lilies. They slipped in gullies created by the rain, but the everlasting memorials kept stiffly to their plastic circles, to their place.

GLEN HUSER

Glen Huser grew up in a small Alberta town northeast
of Edmonton. After two years in education at the
University of Alberta, he began teaching in Edmonton.
Breaks from teaching were taken to attend the Vancouver School of Art and to return to the University of
Alberta where he completed a B.Ed and an M.A. in
English. His focus on English allowed him the oppor-
tunity to study creative writing under Rudy Wiebe,
Margaret Atwood and W.O. Mitchell. Awarded the first
prize in three of the Edmonton *Journal* literary com-
petitions, his stories have appeared in *Dandelion* and
Prism International. In 1978, he developed *Magpie,* a
magazine of student writing and graphics, as a
research project for Edmonton Public Schools. Continuing as managing editor of *Magpie,* he is currently a
consultant in learning resources for Edmonton Public
Schools and is often involved in writing workshops.
Huser lives in Edmonton with his son, Casey, and a
precocious dog, Bartholomew.

NeWest Press launched the Nunatak Fiction Series in 1989 with Joan Crate's outstanding novel, *Breathing Water*. Glen Huser's *Grace Lake* is the second book in the series. NeWest plans to publish at least one new Nunatak book each year.

What critics said about the first Nunatak. . . .

The Calgary Herald:

> "Sexy and sensual and evocative, *Breathing Water* is a character novel, a decidedly literary work. . . . "

The Edmonton Journal:

> "*Breathing Water* seems an excellent 'first Nunatak' choice: it is a poetic, demanding novel; it embraces the idea of story even as it tells one, emphasizing that story is crucial to identity, to being."

The Halifax *Daily News Sunday Magazine*:

> "Joan Crate is a new writer who deserves attention. *Breathing Water*, her fiction debut. . . . , and the novel chosen by NeWest to launch its Nunatak Fiction series, is a heady mix of passion, humor, angst, and poetic display."

Books in Canada:

> "Crate's handling of her characters is deft and insightful: *Breathing Water* is an impressive addition to the ranks of madding-woman novels."